CIRCUS OF
THE LOST

KEN NOBLES

First Edition 2020 ISBN: 978-0-9909471-8-9

Cover Design by Dan Pitts

Published in the United States of America

PAINTED QUILL
PUBLISHING

This book is dedicated to all the strong, smart, caring women I've known throughout my life. I hope you see fragments of your influence mirrored in these pages and that you're proud of the reflection.

ACKNOWLEDGMENTS

Circus of the Lost has been an idea I've had for a while, and it's exciting to see it finally become a reality. Ideas are all unique. Some form quickly and easily while others, like those in the book you're holding now, have to be worked like taffy – stretched and twisted and pulled until it looks the way taffy should. I hope you enjoy this story. I have attempted to create simplistic depth while telling a tale of love, pain, and betrayal with which readers of all ages can relate.

I want to say a special "thank you" to those of you who have read my previous books! You are so important to me, and I always do my best to provide you with exciting, enjoyable content. First of all, I write because God gifted me with the ability to do so. Secondly, I do it for you. And if Circus of the Lost is the first book of mine you're reading – welcome! I'm especially proud of this one.

I'd also like to thank Dan Pitts who has provided the art-work for all of my books so far. He is amazing to work with and truly seeks to understand each project. Even though my vision can be muddled at times, Dan always manages to find the right look. I hope there will be many more covers to come.

Thank you, DeeAnn Day, for the excellent editing and notes. You worked quickly and thoroughly and you deserve credit for helping shape this book. It was a true pleasure having you read my work and hear your thoughts.

Thank you to my test readers. I appreciated every note and comment provided. Reader input is a vitally important part of the writing process for me, and you guys helped me tremendously. Also, I must thank Jordan Diomede for talking this story through with me and helping me create an absolute mess my characters and I will have to struggle with for at least a couple of more books. Your insight and willingness to brainstorm is much appreciated.

As always, thank you to my family who has provided me with a great amount of material and ideas over the years. Your excitement for my writing makes things especially fun for me. And a huge thank you to my wife, Gretchen. She is my sounding board, my first draft critic, and my greatest champion. Your words carry a lot of weight for me and I value your advice. Besides, you're usually right, aren't you?

CHAPTER ONE

IT HAD BEEN nearly two years since I'd become one of The Lost. I was plucked right out of my life and given a new one. Not that it bothered me. There's a saying I've heard: "Friends are the family you choose." While there must be some truth to that, it certainly wasn't the case for me. My family had always been chosen for me. Friends too. But honestly, I don't think I ever really understood the concept of family. I suppose that was to be expected. It was simply one of the benefits of being a VIP member of the government foster care program. Having lived in eight different homes by my fifteenth birthday, it became difficult to define *normal.* I'd become comfortable with instability. But that was all in the past, before I was collected. My life changed quickly after that. As soon as The Collector found me and took me in, my family and friends became one in the same, and I had no complaints about my new reality. Not in the beginning. Although…I often wondered if I ever had any choice in the matter. It seemed to me that choice had always been an illusion. Like watching a jaw dropping act at the circus — one that left you with the feeling anything was possible. Even when you knew it wasn't.

The Lost. It's what they called us at the circus and how they introduced us to the crowds of cheering fans. Which was somewhat ironic since it was the only time in my young life that I didn't feel lost. I felt more a part of something than I ever had in my life. Traveling with the circus had been a strange thing to get used to and difficult to explain. It was a challenge to help someone understand what it's like to wake up one morning in first century Rome and the next in 1985 Los Angeles. It was bizarre and fascinating and occasionally a bit unnerving. Some of us considered it an honor to serve in The Collector's mystical circus, while others viewed it as a curse. I hadn't completely decided. There were days I felt like I belonged to something special. I had the opportunity to travel through space and time, meeting interesting people and visiting the most amazing places. It was magical. A life most people could never dream of having. But other times, usually late at night when I couldn't sleep, I felt alone. Out of place. Lost.

All of those thoughts were flickering through my mind like fireflies, zipping in and out of my consciousness. I crouched behind a white van and stared up toward the second floor window of the perfect little house in front of me. It was growing dark out, and I had strategically chosen my spot, just out of reach of the streetlight's glow. A gauzy curtain of mist hung in the air, and the street beneath me gleamed with a thin coat of drizzle. A pale, white light shone through the window above, creating a soft silhouette of the girl who sat there reading.

Sophia.

As I knelt there, lost in the quiet of that moment, a warm

sensation spread across my left ear, quickly evolving into a searing scorch. Instinctively, I reached back and swatted my friend's hand away. "Cut it out, Ember."

"Are you still stalking that girl?" Ember asked as she sat down on the street next to me. "You could get arrested for that, you know?"

Ember was a fellow member of the circus and the first friend I'd made upon arriving. Ember wasn't her real name. It was more of a stage name that managed to stick. Most members with an ability had a stage name or a nickname. And, as The Collector would nightly introduce her, Ember was, *The Master of Fire and the Tamer of Flames.* She was one of the featured acts — a show that sold out no matter the time or place. From the start, Ember and I got along well. I was always a bit reserved and Ember was anything but. I admired her for that. It was impressive how she did or said whatever she wanted and how she carried herself like she never had a single doubt about anything. Her outlook on life was a perfect match to her unique skill, and her fire engine red hair grabbed peoples' attention almost as quickly as her boldness.

Members of The Collector's Circus basically came in two varieties. Evos and Primes. Ember was a Prime, those who demonstrated special abilities early on, some from birth. Evos developed their abilities later. Usually by their early teens. I was an Evo. An Evo who hadn't manifested. In a way it was embarrassing, especially being surrounded by such amazing people with such impressive abilities. But Olivia, The Collector's Seer and ability trainer, was certain I would manifest and told me it could happen any day. I had serious doubts.

"I'm not stalking her," I said without looking away from the window. "I'm just…checking in on her."

Ember huffed and turned up the corner of her lip. "Oh. You're checking in on her. Only she doesn't know you're here. Or that you exist. Or that you love her."

"I don't love her," I said a little louder than I'd intended. Trying to make myself smaller, I pulled in close to the van. Ember didn't budge. "And she does know I exist. We were friends."

"Friends who haven't spoken in two years." She paused and I could feel her eyes on me. "I forgot, how exactly do you know each other?"

"I've told you this like a thousand times," I said, finally turning my attention to Ember. "We went to school together for a while. We were good friends, but then I got moved to a different home and had to change schools. We lost touch."

"She's cute," Ember said. I didn't respond. "Can we go now? We only have an hour and I want one of those latte things before we go back. We're only able to get them like twice a year."

"And how do you plan to pay for your *latte thing?*"

"With this," she said, holding up a ten dollar bill.

"Where did you get that?"

"You see that fancy car?" Ember pointed to a shiny black vehicle parked across the street. "It was in the…what do you call it? Cup holder?"

"So, you stole it?"

Ember looked at me as if she was astounded at my stupidity. "Well, yeah. How else would I have ten dollars?"

"Ember, you can't just take things that don't belong —"

"Yeah, yeah, I get it," Ember said with a groan. "If it makes you feel better, I'll put the change back when we're done. Can we just go now?"

I stood and took one last look at Sophia before reluctantly agreeing. "Sure. Let's go."

A few minutes later, Ember and I were sitting at an outdoor table sipping warm lattes and constantly checking the time. The cloudy mist had cleared a bit and there was a slight chill in the air. We loved being outside of the circus. To see people walking, driving, running. Moving. Ember and I never understood where all those people were going or why they seemed to be in such a hurry, but it didn't stop us from trying to figure it out. We sat at the table picking out different people and making up stories about who they were or what their lives were like.

The thin man with the long, dark coat and matching hat was obviously a spy. He quickly weaved through the regulars who moved clumsily along the sidewalk, pausing only long enough to drop a wadded up piece of paper in the trash as he passed. Probably a note for the next spy who'd come behind him.

We decided the young man and woman at the table next to us were on their first date. They had met online and she had a rather large collection of action figures. Her soon to be boyfriend was into gardening and had a killer crop of cherry tomatoes this season. At least that's how it was in our minds.

"So, can I ask a question?" Ember said.

"Umm…sure," I answered. "But since when do you need permission?"

Ember ignored my comment. "Why don't you ever go

up to the girl's house and ring the doorbell? Say, 'Hello? Remember me? How are things going?' It's kind of creepy to just hide behind a van and stare into her bedroom."

I shrugged. "What do you care?"

"I'm just asking," Ember said, raising her eyebrows and taking another sip of her latte.

"Well, when you tell me your secrets, I'll tell you mine."

"Secrets?"

"Yeah, like where are you from?" I said. "*When* are you from? Did you have a family? What was your life like before this?"

I wasn't sure, but I thought I saw the spark of a flame dance in her eyes as Ember stood quickly and shoved her chair under the table. "We're going to be late. Let's go."

"Hey, Ember, I'm sorry."

"Forget it," she said with a fake smile. "We're good. Stare into girls' bedrooms all you want."

"Really, I am sorry. I don't know why I don't just try to talk to her. I guess I don't know what to say."

Her smile slowly became genuine. "How about, 'Hey, you want to run off with me to join a circus of time-traveling freaks?'"

"I'll keep that in mind."

Ember and I raced through the neighborhood streets on our way back to the once vacant lot where the circus stood. The streets were still wet and it was completely dark out with only small pools of light puddling beneath street lamps. Time was running short, so we moved quickly, and soon found ourselves standing atop a bluff at the back of the Pine Hills subdivision, looking down on the well-lit circus grounds.

A large, circular, black and white striped tent stood in the center of the lot with several smaller tents surrounding it. Lights had been strung throughout the entire area, bathing the circus in a ghostly glow. Within the gates, people moved about urgently, finishing up preparations for opening night. We were cutting it close.

"Hey, what are you two doing?" a man's voice called. Ember and I turned at once to see a nicely dressed man stepping out of a shiny, black car. A car that once contained a ten dollar bill.

"Nothing, sir," I answered. "We're just walking through."

He stepped toward us. "You're from that circus, aren't you?" The way he said it, the look on his face; it was like he was staring at a couple of cockroaches that had skittered out into the light. "You shouldn't be in this neighborhood. There's nothing here for you to steal, so just keep —"

"Excuse me?" Ember said. "You think we're trying to steal from you?"

He was upon us quickly, puffed up and red-faced. "All I know is, you little weirdos show up and things start missing."

"Come on," I said, taking Ember by the arm. "Let's get out of here."

Ember jerked free of my grip and narrowed her eyes at the man. "Why don't you turn around and walk away before someone gets hurt."

The man called back to his wife. "Honey…" The woman was standing in their driveway with her phone at the ready. "Call the police, will you? It looks like we have a problem here."

"We don't have time for this," Ember said as she turned

to leave. The man raced forward and took hold of her wrist and my heart sank. It was a terrible mistake. "Get your hands off me," E mber said through gritted teeth.

He tightened his grasp. "You're not going anywhere till the police get here."

I tried to step in, but Ember reacted much faster than I'd anticipated. Three things happened nearly at once. Ember yelled something unintelligible, her eyes burned crimson red, and a visible wave of heat shot from her body. The man's hand, which was firmly latched onto Ember's bare skin, was instantly scorched. There was a sizzling sound, a blast of smoke, and the stench of burning flesh. The well-dressed gentleman pulled his hand free, glaring in horror at his bloody, blackened palm. He stumbled backwards before being overtaken by a second blast of heat and smoke that knocked him flat on his back against the wet pavement.

With a terrified scream, his wife frantically punched numbers on her phone. "Hello? Hello?" she said, shaking.

"Put it away," Ember called out as she marched past the woman's squirming husband. His wife made a break toward the open doorway. "I said, put it away." And with a wave of Ember's hand the phone instantly melted in the woman's grasp. With one final scream, she threw the phone aside, raced into her home, and slammed the door.

I reached for Ember's hand to help shake her from her angry trance, and immediately regretted it. It felt like I'd grabbed a red hot iron, and I pulled away with a yelp. "I'm sorry, Chase," Ember said, suddenly realizing she had hurt me.

"Don't worry about it. We have to get out of here. Now."

And with those words, Ember and I raced away down the bluff toward the circus, leaving the man in the suit writhing in pain on the asphalt and his terrified wife hiding inside their home.

"That was stupid, Ember. You better hope that guy and his wife don't come looking for us," I said as we ran.

"Oh, please," Ember said. "Did you see the look on his face? On her face? They wouldn't dare come looking for us. They'll both have nightmares for weeks."

It was at that moment when I felt the prickle on the back of my neck. I slapped my hand over the mark. "Ember, did you feel that? Your mark?"

She reached up and touched the back of her own neck. "Well *now* I do. Don't worry though. We're nearly there."

Each member of the circus had a permanent mark on their neck. It was like a tattoo, except it was placed there by The Collector's assistant, Analise. I met her the first night I arrived — the night I got my mark. She simply rested her hand on my neck and branded the symbol into my skin. It wasn't as painful as it sounds though. It stung for a minute, but the sensation quickly passed, leaving behind a diamond shaped mark with a half-moon in the center. I don't know exactly what the mark does, but there are two things I know for sure. When it tingles, Analise is looking for you. And, on her command, the mark allows her to cut off the abilities of each and every one of us. For me it didn't mean much since I hadn't manifested, but the others hated it. Ember said it felt like she had a light bulb inside that got switched off.

"This way. Quickly," a voice called from behind the fence. It was Setu, a security guard and close friend. Setu was a

Prime, originally from Punjab, India, a city called Batala, somewhere around the early 1930s. He was a large man, clearly strong, with a pleasant nature and a rather unique ability. Setu worked security, except when he's helped out with special projects for The Collector. Having the ability to disappear and reappear at will, Setu was an asset in many ways.

"There," Ember said, pointing to a gap in the fence. A tall chain link fence surrounded the circus grounds anytime between 1910 and the present. A thick, gray tarp lined the inside of the fence to keep the mysteries within separated from the eyes of those who couldn't afford to pay.

"Hurry, they're looking for you," Setu said. With strong hands he pulled the fence up, creating a gap that Ember and I scrambled through.

"Thank you, Setu," I said once we were safely inside. "We owe you."

"You certainly do," Setu replied. His voice was kind and his eyes gentle, but there was a hint of aggravation there. "You cut it close this time. Do you know what they'd do to me if they found out I was helping you sneak away?"

Ember answered immediately. "They'd probably put you in the hole for a week."

Setu shook his head. "The hole is for you younger folk. Those of us in security don't get sent to the hole when we fail The Collector. We join the Forsaken."

"We're really sorry, Setu," I said. "We won't ever do that to you again."

Ember placed her hand on Setu's arm. "And we would never let you become a Forsaken. You're our friend."

The mark on my neck practically buzzed, and from the way Ember's hand went to her own neck, I assumed she felt it as well.

"I have to get to costumes," Ember said as she sprinted away.

"And you have a session," Setu said to me. "Ms. Olivia is a very busy woman. Do not keep her waiting, Chase."

I had gotten no more than a few steps away when Setu called to me again. "We're you able to see her? The girl?"

"I did."

"And was she as lovely as you remember?" Without knowing how to answer the question, I simply nodded. Setu stepped toward me, wiping his dark forehead with the back of his hand. "I had a girl once," he said as his eyes moved to the ground and back. "Before all of this. You are fortunate we return here each year. Make the most of it, young one. When the opportunity presents itself again, speak to the girl. No one should live with regrets."

CHAPTER TWO

OLIVIA HAD BEEN with the circus longer than any of us. She was an odd woman, always looking at you like she was trying to solve some annoying puzzle. I assumed it was a natural expression for someone with a job such as hers. Olivia was a Seer. There are a few different types of Seers, but she was what circus members referred to as a Soul Seer. A vitally important position, it was Olivia's responsibility to work with Evos who had yet to manifest — people like me. She would dig around inside of our minds to discover our abilities and bring them to the surface. For some it happened quickly, in just a session or two. With others, again, like me, things didn't happen so easily. I'd met with Olivia twice a week for nearly two years, and I was no closer to understanding my ability than I was on day one. The sessions had become more intense as the months dragged on. More intrusive. I could see Olivia's frustration, and I was afraid that if I didn't manifest soon, I might be forced to leave the circus. No one had ever said such things to me, but I felt it all the same.

"Come in, Chase," Olivia said sharply. "You're late as it is. The Collector will be gathering everyone soon, so we need to get started."

"Yes, ma'am," I said as I took a seat. Olivia pulled up a chair in front of mine and sat down facing me. Everything about the woman was harsh and prickly. From her angular chin, to her sharp nose and razor-like personality, Olivia was all business.

"I want to begin a bit further back than usual," Olivia said as she clicked her pen open and began scribbling on a legal pad. "I'd like to see if we can tap into your earliest memories."

"Okay," I said as I picked at my thumbnail. I hated those sessions. The thought of someone poking around in my head made me feel like a defenseless little lab mouse. Honestly, I don't know why I felt that way. It's not like Olivia had ever hurt me. If anything, I suppose I was embarrassed by what she might find. Things or feelings I'd rather keep hidden. Although I wasn't sure what those would be. And I figured if Olivia had any idea Ember and I had been sneaking away, she would have reported it long ago. Ember said I shouldn't worry about it. That it wasn't the kind of thing Olivia was looking for. But Ember never seemed to worry about much, so I couldn't totally trust her judgment.

"Close your eyes now and concentrate," Olivia began. I did as she asked and closed my eyes just as her index finger pressed against my forehead. "I want you to picture yourself as an infant. Tiny. A newborn." She paused. "Breathe, now. Let your mind go. I want you to feel your hunger. Hear your cries. Sense your mother's touch. Search for her voice."

In an instant, my body went numb and my mind felt as if it had pulled away from my body. I traveled all the way back to when I was just a baby lying in a crib. My eyes worked, but everything was fuzzy and all I could focus on were the bright colors of my blanket and the soft, stuffed toys lying around me. There was noise. I was crying. I needed something. Was it food? No. Sleep? No, I was wide awake. Did I need to be changed? I wasn't sure, but I didn't think so.

I heard a woman's voice. It was kind. Loving. "What are you fussing about?" A figure appeared above me. A woman with long, dark hair that fell around her face as she peeked into my crib. I'm not sure how, maybe it was her voice, but I immediately knew she was my mother.

It was the first time in my life I'd seen or heard her. I had grown up in the homes of strangers for as long as I could remember, and none of them ever gave me any information about my mother or father. Addicts. That's what the social worker told me when I was old enough to ask questions. They were addicts who eventually lost their lives to their addiction.

"Come here, sweet boy," the woman said. I felt her hands wrap around me and then I was rising from my crib and into her arms. She pulled me in close. She was warm and smelled like flowers. I was safe. My crying stopped and I felt comfort like I had never felt in my life, and never felt since. I pulled my wobbly head back and stared into her face, but again I had trouble focusing. I could make out her eyes, nose, teeth, and hair, but none of it came together to form a clear picture. It was like I was staring at her through a sheet of cobwebs. No matter how much I strained or squinted, I couldn't force her image into focus. Then Olivia's voice cut through.

"Tell me what you wanted, Chase. Why were you crying? Why did you stop?"

I was still staring into my mother's blurry face when I

heard my own voice call out, the sound coming from some-where inside of me. "I wanted her. I needed her."

"Why did you need her?"

"I was — I was afraid."

"Afraid of what?"

I searched my mind, looking for the words. "I don't know."

"Think, Chase," Olivia said, her voice like a whip. "It's important. What were you afraid of?"

"I don't know," I said. "I just knew she would protect me. That she would make sure nothing bad happened to me. She would cover me. Hide me."

"Hide you from what?"

"Nothing," I said. "Everything."

Olivia snapped. "Be specific."

"I was afraid something would hurt me." Just then, my mother grabbed the blanket from my crib, covered me up and pulled me in even tighter. "I don't what I was afraid of, but I knew she would keep me safe. If she held me, it couldn't see me. It couldn't find me."

And instantly, Olivia pulled me from the vision. I opened my eyes to see Olivia already moving from her chair back to her desk. "That's all for today," she said.

"Was that my mother?" I asked, even though I knew the answer. "The woman in my dream?"

"It wasn't a dream. It was a memory. And yes, it was your mother."

"Can you tell me about her?" I asked as I stood. "I don't know anything about her. Do you know her name? Do you know where we lived?"

Olivia sighed and dropped into the chair behind her desk. "I only know she was your mother because *you* knew she was your mother. I can't know anything more or less than you. I untangle your thoughts and interpret your memories, filling in the blanks as best as I can. But I'm not all-knowing."

"I understand," I said. Honestly, I didn't expect her to tell me anything. There was a time when being kept in the dark made me angry. Growing up, all I wanted to know was where I came from and who I was before I was alone. I had grown accustomed to unanswered questions that left me feeling hollow and lost. Living with that emptiness was familiar for me.

Olivia paused and stared at me long enough for the silence to become uncomfortable. "We're running out of time, Chase."

"Am I late?" I asked, glancing around the room for a clock. "Are the gates opening?"

Olivia shook her head. "What I mean is, if I don't discover your ability soon…"

"He'll let me go."

"The Collector has given me a deadline and we're coming up on it quickly," she said. "I've asked him to reconsider because I know something is there. I can feel it. There's something powerful in you. But if I can't draw it out, he will lose patience. I need you to take these sessions seriously. I know you don't enjoy them, but I need you to try. Try to work with me."

I nodded. "I understand. I'll try."

"For your sake, I hope so," Olivia said as she scribbled some notes on the legal pad. "Go now. You have work to do."

It was a long standing tradition for all circus members to gather at the main tent on opening night. The Collector would give a speech before unlatching the gates and allowing the delighted guests to enter. Ember and I stood together in the gathering crowd of performers and crew members waiting for the moment The Collector would appear. He would speak, the gates would be thrown open, and the night would begin.

"Did you get yelled at?" Ember asked. "Was Olivia mad at you?"

"I didn't get yelled at, but things were different this time."

Ember's forehead wrinkled. "Different, how?"

"She seemed upset. Like I was going to be in big trouble if she couldn't figure out my ability soon."

"I wouldn't worry," Ember said with a shrug. "She'll figure it out. It's her job."

"But what if —"

"Don't even say it. Things will be fine."

"But seriously," I added as my voice jumped an octave. "What if they're wrong? What if I'm not an Evo at all? What if The Collector is —" I glanced around and lowered my voice. "What if The Collector made a mistake? Maybe I don't have any abilities at all."

Ember shook her head and had no more than opened her mouth to answer when she was abruptly interrupted. "What's up, guys?" a young boy said as he raced up. He accidentally bumped into Ember, nearly knocking her over. "Oh, sorry. I was running."

"Yeah," Ember said, angrily dusting off her costume. "We noticed."

It was our friend, Echo. At least, I guess you'd call him our friend. We didn't know his real name; he never told us and we never thought to ask. He was just Echo. The name fit. He was friendly and loyal but a strange boy nonetheless. Something was always slightly off balance and awkward about Echo. He loved ketchup, provided anyone who'd listen with random information about animals, and always greeted everyone with a handshake. However, what Echo lacked in social skills he more than made up for with his technical brilliance. He was a Seer, similar to Olivia, but his skills were very different. Echo could literally feel his way through anything mechanical or technical. It was amazing to watch. Anytime something at the circus was broken or not functioning properly, Echo was the first call. He never actually repaired anything, but simply by laying his hands on an object, he could tell you what was wrong with it.

I saw one of the stagehands bring him a pocket watch once. It had stopped working and the man was terribly upset. Apparently, it was a family heirloom. Echo took the watch, held it firmly in his hands, and almost immediately replied, "There's a busted spring. It should be repairable though." The man smiled, hugged Echo, and raced away. Inspired by the embrace, Echo then went on to explain to us in great detail about how various animals show affection within their own species and how they do so with humans. Apparently chimpanzees are the only animals, other than humans, who give hugs.

Echo was invaluable to The Collector. When the circus

would visit the modern world, Echo used the one and only computer to scour the Internet in hopes of locating potential members for the circus. Based on the information he gathered, The Collector would travel to a particular place and time to find the individual Echo had targeted. Many times, the stories he'd discover about humans with abilities were just tall tales with little or no connection to reality. But sometimes Echo would uncover a person with true power. Real abilities. The Collector would then recruit, or attempt to recruit, that person to join the circus. Echo was very good at his job, and many people were a part of the circus because he had found them.

"You have to be careful, Echo," Ember snapped. "One day you're going to bump into me, scare me, and end up getting your ears burned off."

"That would be unfortunate," Echo said, with a strained laugh. He blinked rapidly. "But I don't have to worry about that now. Your powers aren't working since Analise —"

"I know they aren't working," Ember said as she threw her head back and groaned. "Everyone knows that."

Echo went on as if he had no idea Ember was annoyed. "Anyway, there's something I need to tell you. Both of you."

"I don't want to hear anything else about penguins," Ember said, rolling her eyes. "We get it. They are *fascinating creatures.*"

Echo chuckled. "They truly are. I'm actually more into cheetahs right now, but it's not about that either."

"Well, it'll have to wait," Ember said. "The Collector's here."

A cheer rose from the crowd as The Collector stepped up

onto a small, wooden stool. He removed his hat, flashed a toothy smile, and beamed with confidence. "Good evening, my friends," he said, throwing his arms out in front of him. I found myself smiling as I watched him greet us. I simply didn't understand how a person could be so comfortable with all eyes on him. He was tall and imposing, a true showman. His suit was crimson red, trimmed in gold with a brilliant white shirt underneath and matching white patent leather shoes. Although he had just removed his hat, his hair was perfect. Thick, wavy brown hair, long on top and shaved close on the sides. He had a tan like someone who'd spent his whole life on the beach, and his thick mustache was trimmed so perfectly it was like he'd just stepped out of a barber's chair.

"You have no idea how much it thrills me to look into your faces this evening," The Collector continued. "And I know you've heard me say those words many times before, but they are no less true tonight than ever before. All of you are special in your own right. Unique. Powerful. Possessing abilities the world can scarcely imagine. But as powerful as we are individually, together is where our true strength lies. Together we are an unstoppable force. In a few moments we will open our gates and allow the good people of this time to behold a spectacle the likes of which they may never see again. But when all is said and done and we close those gates at the end of the week, I want them to leave feeling something more than awe. I would consider it a failure if they returned home only to muse about the amazing feats they witnessed here. Rather, I want them to speak of the joy they felt within these grounds. I want them to recall the feeling of wonder. And most importantly, I want them to think of you. Not you as individuals, but you as one. Not a circus of performers. Not the incredible things we can do. No. All of that is secondary. I want them to think of you first as a family. The family they all dream of having. A family of men and women, boys and girls who love one another. Who respect one another. Who would die for one another. This circus is not your job. This circus is not your responsibility. This circus is your family."

We all reveled at The Collector's words. We were one — a nomadic tribe of like-minded individuals trumpeting our support. Over the last two years, I had heard similar speeches, but that night felt different. I wanted to believe him. I needed to feel a part of something. I wanted to believe I belonged — that I mattered. That anything was possible. I'd seen firsthand the amazing things our people could do. There was truly nothing we couldn't accomplish if we worked together. If we could be one. If we were the family The Collector wanted us to be. He was our leader, and we were his people. We were happy to follow him throughout space and time to keep his dream alive.

The Collector placed his hat upon his head and called out in a great, booming voice, "Now, for the lighting of the cauldron." Again, our cheers rose as one. "Analise, if you will, please liberate the abilities of these fine men and women."

There were two individuals who never left The Collector's side, and that day was no different. Luka and Analise. Luka was The Collector's bodyguard, large and imposing. We all assumed his ability was superior strength, but that was only a guess. The mystery of the hulking man was even more frightening than his blank stare and mammoth build.

He reminded me of a human boulder. Slow moving and powerful, with a face that looked as if it had been chipped out of granite.

Then there was Analise, a Suppressor and the first person each new recruit met upon arrival. I clearly remember the first night I was brought in. Analise greeted me with an icy stare and a disinterested welcome. She was easily the most intimidating person I'd ever met, with hair as white as snow and skin so fair it practically glowed. Analise was the one responsible for the mark on the back of our necks. A faint spark would shimmer in her cold, blue eyes, and the air would crackle with energy whenever she would release us from her hold. *It was for our own safety,* The Collector would say. *And the safety of the circus.* Rarely had I ever heard Analise speak and when I did it was usually in hushed tones aimed at The Collector's ear.

The Collector scanned the crowd until he found the face of the one he needed. "Ember," he called aloud when he'd located her. "Will you please do us the honor of lighting the Cauldron of Kinship so that we may begin the evening's festivities?"

Ember stepped away from the crowd, lifted her hands, and focused her attention on the large, brass cauldron. In a matter of seconds, the pile of wood within the shallow bowl blazed to life, cracking and popping under the intense heat. Golden flames roared to life, pushing out against the fading twilight. Ember took her place with the rest of us, a proud smile on her face.

"Everyone, take your positions," The Collector bellowed as we scrambled in all directions. "Guards, open the gates and let the people come. May we all be who we were born to be."

CHAPTER THREE

FOR ALL OF the amazing things that happened at the circus on a nightly basis, I had possibly the worst job. I picked up trash. I wandered around the grounds in a yellow vest with a plastic bag and a poky stick cleaning up after people who couldn't manage to use a trash can. Popcorn boxes, empty drink containers, and discarded ticket stubs were my specialty, but occasionally I'd have the pleasure of cleaning up someone's spilled nachos or ant-covered turkey legs. Things were simpler when we were set up in earlier years. Food wasn't always a part of the festivities in our more archaic venues, unless it was an event for royalty or nobles. But in good old modern America, my job was clear. Keep the grounds clean. The Collector said that my job was vitally important in order to maintain the fantasy. To keep people lost in the moment — the experience. Mystery mixed with fantasy was a tough sell if patrons had to stop and scrape gum off of their shoes.

Truth be told, I didn't mind the job too much. For me, it was simply nice to be where everything was happening. To be a part of something. And I always held on to the hope that soon my ability would manifest and I could move on to doing something different. Something less messy. Maybe I could even be in a show like Ember.

I propped my poker up beside the tent and stared up at the perfect October sky. The clouds had begun to clear but were still scattered across the horizon like tattered, black sails. Stars were peeking through the sheets of torn sky and a full, yellow moon was pushing away what was left of the fading gloom. It was cool out — chilly almost. As a result, people weren't eating as much, but there was a record number of discarded cocoa cups littered along the walking trails.

That night in Atlanta was one I'd easily remember for the rest of my life. It was the first night I saw the mysterious man in the green bow tie. I'd see him two more times before actually speaking to him, but for years afterward, I wondered how many nights he'd been there at the circus without anyone knowing. How long had he been watching? Planning? Waiting for the right moment.

No matter how busy I was, I always tried to make sure I caught Ember's show. She never asked me to be there, and even though she wouldn't admit it, I knew it was important to her. It was like a ritual for us. I'd watch her show, the circus would close for the evening, and we'd sit around the fire talking late into the night.

It was easy for me to duck in just after her show began. The grounds were relatively empty and the food stalls and gaming booths would close for the night as soon as her act began. There was no reason for them to stay open. No one wanted to miss the girl of fire. Ember's show typically sold out no matter when or where we were, which made it easier for me to be there supporting her. The crowd that gathered in the main tent was large enough no one even gave me a second glance. All I had to do was remove my vest and blend in.

The Collector's muffled voice welcomed Ember to the stage and I scooted in just before the room went black. The tent was filled with the murmur of excitement. I loved the modern shows. Ember never failed to entertain, but add in lights and music, and the show was breathtaking. There was a deep rumble and a boom just as the spotlight flashed to life and cut through the darkness. Ember stood alone center stage, arms pressed to her side, legs together, head down. Soft strings began to play and it felt as if we all collectively held our breath. With a gentle flick of her wrists, sparks flew from Ember's hands filling the entire tent with what looked like millions of fireflies dancing above our heads. As the strings played on, the sparks flooded the tent, circling, rising, and falling as if they were somehow connected to the rhythm. They shimmered and blinked in time — a choreographed dance. The music picked up and began to pulse as the sparks dissolved into the darkness. Ripples of flame emanated from Ember with each throbbing beat of the drum. She prowled the stage like a tiger as the music swelled, the pulsing bursts of fire matching its intensity.

Then suddenly there was silence. The spotlight shut off, and the room was plunged into darkness. There was a brief lull filled with audible gasps before music blared through the silence and an inferno of flames lit up the main tent. When the house lights came on, we saw Ember standing high above the stage on a scaffolding, shooting a torrent of flames in all directions. Applause broke out in a tidal wave of shouts and cheers.

Located along the perimeter of the main tent, on both sides of the stage, was more scaffolding with men perched atop. They crouched behind over-sized red cannons, all aimed at Ember. One by one the men fired off their cannons in time with the music, sending sparkling silver cannonballs careening toward her. Ember shot fireball after fireball, connecting with each of the cannonballs as they soared over the crowd. Flame and tin collided and the cannonballs exploded into various colors of smoke and fire. Red, yellow, blue, green — one by one they thundered overhead. The adults roared with delight, and the children covered their ears and squealed with nervous excitement until eventually the cannon fire ceased and the music fell. It was quiet again. Soft strings resumed and Ember again stood still in near silence.

The lights dimmed and a hazy glow formed around Ember. At first it was no more than a faint orange shimmer, but soon the light intensified and heat began to rise from her body in thin, translucent waves. The haze grew and swelled, morphing from orange, to yellow, to white. It swirled around her, drawing in glowing particles as it spun faster and faster. Soon, the heat and light swirled so rapidly it hardly looked as if it was swirling at all. It transformed. Changed into a living, breathing creature. Light and heat came to life, surrounding its master. Protecting her. With a flash, the air around her ignited into flame. And from that spinning cocoon of fire a shape appeared. The massive head of a tiger, snarling and snapping its fiery fangs. It lunged out over the crowd, a deadly beast filling nearly the entire tent. Men, women, and children were forced to shield themselves from its scorching fury. When the heat was nearly too much to bear, the beast suddenly retreated back into the swirling mass surrounding Ember and was gone.

Music swelled once more and with it, Ember's feet left the scaffolding as she slowly rose toward the ceiling of the tent. Waves of heat pushed her upward as she hovered over the people, arms spread wide, cords of fire spinning around her. After making a full pass around the tent, Ember slowly descended until she hovered just a few feet above the stage. With one last surge, the music rose and quickly ended as the fire surrounding her blasted outward. With a flash, Ember disappeared leaving nothing but a smoky silhouette of herself on the stage. There was a moment of hushed awe before the crowd erupted in applause.

"Thank you for being part of our family tonight," The Collector said as he took the stage. "I hope you've enjoyed being here as much as we have enjoyed being your hosts. This ends our festivities for the evening. Goodnight, and may time be kind to you." With those words, the men, women, and children poured out of the tent, excitedly recounting the details of the performance they'd just witnessed.

I was among the first to leave the main tent that night, and as I stepped out into the grounds I saw him. The man in the green bow tie. Normally I may not have thought anything of it, but there was something odd about him. The way he stood there alone in the middle of the pathway staring at me. I got the feeling he had been waiting for me. For a moment we stood there, eyes locked, until someone bumped into me and I glanced away. When I looked back, he was gone. I brushed it off at the time. I had enough concerns battling for my attention. Besides, work was over, and it was my favorite part of the night.

❧

"I almost missed the second one," Ember said as she jabbed at the campfire with a stick. Sparks fluttered out and disappeared into the night sky. "Barely just clipped the bottom of it."

"It didn't look that way to me," I said. "But what if you did miss? Are those things heavy? Would it hurt if one of them hit you?"

"I don't know how heavy they are, but I'm pretty sure anything getting shot out of a cannon would hurt if it hit you."

"It might hurt, but it probably wouldn't kill you," Echo said as he walked up and sat down too close to Ember for her liking. She frowned and inched away. "Hey, Chase." Echo reached over Ember to shake my hand. "Hey, Ember." He grinned and offered his hand to her as well. Ember sighed and granted him an unenthusiastic handshake before pulling away. "The cannonballs are made out of a lightweight aluminum fixed around a balsa wood frame. The loud booming sounds are merely for effect. Any damage they'd do would be superficial at best. Unless, of course, it hit you in the face. Then you'd run the risk of it breaking your nose or even damaging your eyes. However, the odds of that are — "

"We get it," Ember said. "They aren't dangerous."

"They are," Echo said with a nervous smile. "Just not gravely so."

After the gates closed for the night, little campfires would pop up around the sleeping tents. As soon as we finished our clean up, the day was officially over and everyone could relax and hang out. Dinner was delivered to us in individual paper bags, and we'd all eat while we talked about our day. I realized discussing our day would sound a little lame to most people, but I liked it. When I was growing up, some of the families I lived with would make us all eat dinner together. They'd try to get us to open up and talk about our lives, what happened at school, or what we wanted to do for the weekend, but it always felt hollow. It wasn't real. It's like we were *playing* family, but I never felt like it was genuine. But here, in the circus, we were a family. We looked out for one another. We loved one another. It was real. Or at least it felt real.

"Tell me about your session with Olivia," Ember said. "How did it go?"

"Okay, I guess." I sat there tearing apart my paper bag, rolling up the pieces, and tossing them into the fire.

Echo cut in. "Oh, that reminds me. I need to talk to you guys about —"

"Hold on, Echo," Ember said, lifting a finger. "What happened? Is everything okay?"

"Everything is fine. It's just…this session was different. I saw my mom. My real mom."

"Chase, that's amazing," Ember said, placing her hand on my arm. "What happened? What was she like? Did she look like you?"

"I don't know. I couldn't really see her," I said. "The memory was from when I really young. A baby. Everything was kind of blurry and confusing. But I know it was her. And I heard her voice."

"That's a big deal," Ember said, wide-eyed. "Did you see anything else? Could you tell where you were?"

I shook my head and turned my attention back to the paper bag in my hands. "No. Olivia wasn't really interested in the part about my mom. She was more worried about how I was feeling. Whether or not I was scared or sad. It was weird."

"Well, I'm sure Olivia has her reasons," Ember said as she resumed her poking at the fire. "She's good at what she does. You'll be manifesting soon. I can feel it."

Echo looked surprised. "You can?"

Ember answered him without missing a beat. "Figure of speech."

"Got it," Echo said, nodding.

"I hope you're right," I said. "But that's not all we talked about. She's worried I might be running out of time."

Ember locked eyes with me. "Running out of time?"

"She said The Collector won't wait much longer. That if something doesn't happen soon, he might —"

"Don't," Ember said. She stood up and tossed the stick into the fire. "It's not going to happen."

It would have been nice to have Ember's confidence. I wished I believed everything would be okay. I wished I could speak with such certainty. "Yeah" was all I managed to say.

"Don't worry," Echo said. "Some people take a long time to manifest. Years even. It'll happen."

"You see there, Chase," Ember said with a smile. "Echo and I agree. What more do you need?"

I smiled even though it seemed forced. "Thanks, guys."

Ember jabbed her head to the side. "Look who it is. Speak of the devil." Olivia was making her way through the camp like a woman on a mission. Her head was down, her steps were quick, and her face was twisted up like she had so many thoughts in her head she didn't know how to keep them contained.

"Hey, Olivia," Ember said as she shot by us. Olivia stopped in her tracks, looked at Ember, then at me. She almost said something but then stopped herself. She simply huffed and raced away.

"Come on," Ember said. "Let's find out where she's going."

I was more than happy to have something to do. Anything was better than continuing that particular conversation. We jumped up and followed Olivia through the circus grounds, keeping a safe distance since we knew Echo would likely be unable to stop talking. He did that when he was nervous. And just as we suspected, he jabbered on nonstop about how this was a bad idea. Soon, Olivia had arrived at The Collector's tent. She paused outside the doorway, took a look around, and ducked inside. Ember turned around to make sure she had Echo's full attention. Her death stare ensured he'd hear every word. "We are going up to that tent, and we're going to listen in on what they're talking about." She placed a finger over Echo's mouth. "You can either keep it zipped, or walk away. Got it?" Echo took a breath and tried to speak, but Ember wouldn't allow it. "Don't say anything. Either nod or just walk away." Echo's eyes darted from Ember to me and back again, but ultimately he nodded and decided to stay with us.

We made our way to the back corner of the tent. Ember seemed to know exactly where to hide to keep us out of view of everyone, but still close enough to hear what was going on inside. We were crouched there in the dark, trying to be as silent as possible. Echo was breathing heavily, but he knew better than to say anything.

"Olivia," The Collector began, "I hope you have good news for me."

"I wish I did, sir. There seems to have been some complications."

"Complications? With Chase?"

Ember and I glanced at one another, and I could see the uneasiness in her eyes. We shouldn't have been there. Sure, I wanted to listen, but I didn't know if I wanted to hear what they were about to say.

"Not exactly," Olivia said. "Chase's session went very well today actually. We're close to something; I just know it."

"You've been saying that for months."

"It was different this time. I believe we had a breakthrough."

"Explain," The Collector said. I heard him sit a heavy glass down on his desk.

"We found a new memory today. We saw Chase's mother."

There was a long pause and my heart pounded so hard I was afraid they might hear it. "And I take it that's a good thing?"

"I believe it is," Olivia said. "With a little more time, I know I'll be able to find out —"

"Time is not an infinite resource, Olivia. You are the best at what you do, but my patience for this matter is beginning to wan. Find out the boy's ability. And do it soon."

"Yes, sir. I - I will." Olivia hesitated. "Sir, there is one more matter I need to discuss with you."

"Go on," The Collector said. I heard his glass scrape across the table as he lifted it.

Echo began tapping my shoulder and wiggling around like he might jump out of his skin. Ember gave him a nudge. "Stop it," she mouthed to him. He reluctantly pulled back and sat there holding his knees and silently rocking.

"It's Chase and Ember," Olivia said. "They left the grounds again today. There was an altercation."

"You know this for certain?"

"Yes, the Seer, Echo, it's all in his report. The police were called."

The glass was slammed down on the table. "Who helped them?"

"I'm not sure, but it seems like we avoided the attention of any outsiders. If the police haven't come by now, I doubt they —"

"Go get them, and bring them to me."

CHAPTER FOUR

AT EIGHT YEARS old I was placed in my third home. There were five kids altogether. We shared two bedrooms — three boys in one and two girls in the other. It was a bitterly cold January morning when my social worker introduced me to Mrs. Marla. I was told it would be a temporary stay, so I went in thinking I'd keep quiet, put my head down, and do whatever she asked. My plan was to survive until I was moved to a permanent family.

Mrs. Marla was a kind lady who was very large, and very much immobile. Most days she could be found lounging in her recliner in the middle of the living room, sipping soda with her feet propped up. She'd call out to us at all hours of the day and night. "My children, come to dinner. My children, do your chores. My children, clean your rooms." And every night, she'd call us downstairs to tell her goodnight and kiss her on the cheek before bed. It was funny that Mrs. Marla referred to us as *her children* because I don't even think she knew our names. She'd given us all nicknames, not even creative ones at that. The tall skinny kid was Slim. The five year old girl was Goldie because of her long, blond hair. Goldie's roommate was a shy little girl with glasses called

Mouse. There was a heavyset boy she called Bear, and then there was me. I suppose nothing struck her as unique as far as I was concerned since, from the moment I arrived, Mrs. Marla deemed me, Newbie.

I lived in the home with Mrs. Marla for six months and during that time, Bear and I became great friends. When it was warm out, we'd be free of the house from morning till night. We'd explore the neighborhood, play basketball on the broken down goal in the front yard, or simply turn on the water hose and create our own backyard water park. But, when the weather wouldn't allow us to be outside, we were forced to get more creative. Mrs. Marla had no television in the house, so Bear and I found other ways to spend our time. Bear had a deck of cards and we'd play Go Fish and talk and laugh for hours. When we weren't playing cards, we'd invent superheros, draw and color them on notebook paper, then cut them out and use them as action figures. We always had a new plan to work out or a new adventure to fuel our imaginations. There was never a boring day with Bear. We'd roll our eyes every time Mrs. Marla barked orders at us from her lounger, interrupting our fun. Though we were careful never to talk back or let her see our frustrations, sometimes we'd sneak into the kitchen late at night and drink her sodas. Payback. Not the mean sort. It was more of the playful variety. Sodas were strictly off limits. Mrs. Marla was adamant they'd stunt our growth, but they hadn't seemed to have that affect on her.

Bear placed a finger to his lips as we tiptoed into the dark kitchen. I was on his heels, my head swiveling to make sure the house was empty and no eyes were on us. Ever so gently,

Bear eased the refrigerator door open. The tearing away of the rubber seal holding it shut sounded like thunder in the silence of that house, and light from the open door flooded the small kitchen. With quiet purposeful movements, Bear reached inside, removed a soda for each of us, handed one to me, and carefully shut the refrigerator door. With a victorious fist bump we turned to leave, but had taken no more than one step back toward our bedroom when Mrs. Marla's deep voice called to us from the darkened living room. "Trying to take my sodas, are you?"

Bear tried to lie, but knew it was no use. "No, Mrs. Marla, we were just…Yes. Yes, we were. I'm sorry."

"And how about you, Newbie? You sorry too?"

I swallowed hard. We couldn't see her sitting there in the dark. She was like a predator hiding in the shadows about to pounce. "Yes, ma'am. I'm sorry too. We'll put them back."

I reached for the refrigerator door. "No," Mrs. Marla said. "Keep them."

"Are you sure, Mrs. Marla?" Bear asked. "We can put them back. We don't want to make you mad."

The lamp beside Mrs. Marla's recliner clicked on, and she sat there staring at us like we were a couple of defenseless lambs. "Me? Mad?" she said. "I'm not mad at all. In fact, I'm glad this happened."

"We really are sorry," Bear said.

"I promise it won't happen again," I added.

Mrs. Marla grunted and sipped her own soda. "You see, I'm not upset because now I finally know what you two really are. Thieves."

Apparently, Bear didn't appreciate the comment. His

tone changed. Like the prey was preparing to strike. "It's just soda. We can put them back."

Mrs. Marla sat up. "It's just soda today. But what will it be tomorrow? Will you steal my food? My tools? Try to rob my safe? How can I ever trust you again?"

"We would never do anything like that," I said. "We didn't think about it as stealing. We just thought —"

"You just thought I'd never know. You just thought that I'm a weak, old woman who'd never miss a couple of sodas. Well, you were wrong, weren't you?" Bear tried to speak, but Mrs. Marla continued. "Take the sodas. Enjoy them. It'll be the last thing you ever steal from me."

The next morning we woke up and got ready as usual. I brushed my teeth, got dressed, and walked out into the living room. Waiting there on the sofa beside Mrs. Marla was my social worker. "It's time to go, Chase," she said, springing to her feet. Her face was tightened up and she was feverishly buttoning her coat. "Go and grab your things." Mrs. Marla sat there with a satisfied smile drawn across her broad face.

"Go? Go where? Did you —" I almost asked if she'd found a home for me. A family. I immediately felt foolish for even thinking it.

She took a deep breath and answered the question I didn't dare ask. "No, Chase. Not yet. But we will. Soon."

I glanced over at Mrs. Marla. She made eye contact for a moment, then took a sip of her soda and turned her head. I left her home that day and never saw Mrs. Marla or Bear again.

∽

"How could you *not* tell us?" Ember yelled at Echo.

Echo shifted around, frantically blinking his eyes. "I'm sorry. I tried to — I tried — I — I —"

"You don't *try* when it comes to something like that," Ember said, red faced. "You don't try, you just do it. You just open your mouth and talk. It's not that hard. Jeeze, Echo, you talk like nonstop. Most of the time I wish you wouldn't, but the one time I really need you to, you say nothing."

"But — but I —"

"It's easy. You just say, Hey Chase, hey Ember, I sold you out when you left the circus earlier today. Sorry."

"I know but —"

"It's alright, Echo," I said. Someone had to save the poor kid. Ember was a challenge for most anyone, but Echo didn't stand a chance.

Ember narrowed her eyes at me. "No. No, it's not alright."

"He didn't do it on purpose, Ember."

"I didn't," Echo managed to say. "I got an alert that the police were called. When that happens, I'm required to —"

"To be a rat," Ember said with a huff.

Echo coughed nervously. "Well, actually, rats get a bad reputation, when in reality they are some of the most impressive —"

"Oh, don't you *dare,*" Ember said lowly, waves of heat radiating from her shoulders.

"You should go, Echo," I said. For once, Echo didn't speak. He knew better. He blinked hard and took off.

"How can you take up for him like that?" Ember fumed.

"You know how Echo is. You know he didn't mean

anything by it. He would never get us in trouble on purpose. He's just...different."

Ember groaned and took a settling breath. "I know. But this is a big deal. What if we end up in the hole? Or worse?"

"Look, we'll just tell them —"

"Ember and Chase," one of the guards interrupted. He'd walked up on us without our noticing. "The Collector would like to see you. Please come with me." We stood there for a moment sharing an anxious glance. For an instant, Ember looked like she might make a run for it, but I guess she changed her mind because with a concerned frown, she stepped right past me and led the way to The Collector's tent.

I had been with the circus for over two years, but it was only the second time I'd set foot in The Collector's tent. The first time was the night he'd come to collect me. As soon as I'd arrived, he introduced me to Analise. She gave me my mark and brought me back to his office. As terrified as I was that night, The Collector managed to put me at ease. He smiled at me like I was a long lost child who had finally returned home. With teary eyes, he stepped up to me, pulled me in close, and hugged me like he'd known me my whole life. Like a father would. "Welcome, Chase," he'd said. "Welcome to the family."

However, something told me my visit with Ember wouldn't be as welcoming as my first. I'd seen people put in the hole before. It was as awful as it sounded. It was literally a hole in the ground. And in that hole was a large cylinder with a drain in the floor to be used as a toilet. Where the cylinder met ground level, there was a set of steel bars, secured with a padlock that stayed locked until The Collector decided to free you. No one was allowed to talk to you or bring you anything. Guards delivered meals, but other than that, people in the hole had no outside contact. Different offenses merited different amounts of time as consequences. If someone missed a work shift, or showed up late for duty, they may be assigned a day in the hole. Last year, two kids got in a fight and were sentenced to five entire days. I'd never known of anyone getting caught sneaking off, so I had no idea what was about to happen. All I knew was, we'd rather end up in the hole than be Forsaken.

"Come in," The Collector said. Ember and I eased into his office. Analise was there as well. Immediately the air became electric and there was a flash in her eyes. I glanced over at Ember and by the grimace on her face, I assumed her abilities had been suppressed. "Do you know why I called for you?"

Ember spoke up first. "Because we left the grounds?"

The Collector nodded, barely acknowledging Ember. He looked directly at me. "And can you explain to me why you decided to leave?"

"It was my fault," I said. "I made Ember come with —"

"No one made me do anything," Ember cut in. "I chose to go. I'm the one who caused the trouble. It was my fault the police were called. This is on me."

The Collector shifted his gaze to Ember, then back to me. "What do you have to say, Chase?"

I stared at my feet for a moment and tried to think of anything I could say that might help us get out of that mess. Of course, nothing came to me. There was no explanation that would make it acceptable for anyone to leave the grounds. It was the number one rule of the circus. So, when nothing came to me, I decided it would be best to go with the truth. "I wanted to see an old friend. Her name is — well she lives near here. Ember came with me because she didn't want me to go alone. If it wasn't for me, Ember wouldn't have left. It was a dumb thing to do, and I'm sorry."

The Collector stepped around his desk and sat down on it, facing us. "And both of you are aware of what happens when circus members break the rules?"

"We are," Ember said. "They're sent to the hole."

"True," The Collector added. "And sometimes worse." He paused, letting those words hang there in the air like a cannonball. "Who helped you?"

Ember spoke up quickly. "No one."

"I would advise you to tell me the truth," The Collector replied in a cool tone. He took a sip from the glass on his desk, and I couldn't help but think of Mrs. Marla and her sodas. "I'm giving you an opportunity. A rather gracious opportunity to be honest. Please don't take my kindness for granted." He paused again, unblinking. When neither of us spoke, he continued. "Tell me, both of you, do you enjoy being a part of this community?"

"Yes," we answered in unison.

"And do you believe that I care for you? That I want what's best for you? What's best for this family?"

"Yes," I said.

Ember wasn't as quick to answer. "Yes," she said finally.

"If what you say is true, it's baffling to me that you'd willingly choose dishonesty. Why would you ever refuse to answer my questions? Surely you understand my priority is to keep you and the other members of the circus safe from the threats that exist beyond our gates."

I glanced over at Ember who was still staring at The Collector. Unflinching. I knew she was scared, but it didn't show. If she felt anything like I did, she was scared to answer his question and scared not to.

"Very well," The Collector said as he stood and made his way back to his chair. "Ember, you may return to your quarters now. Chase, I'll need you to stay with me."

"Sir," Ember said, "I'll take whatever punishment you think I deserve. I know he said it was, but this wasn't all Chase's fault. In fact, I'm probably more to blame since I… attacked someone."

The Collector scratched his chin. "Ember, if I decide that punishment is in order, I will let you know. For now, I need to speak with Chase in private. I appreciate your concern for your friend, but unless you have something more to share with me…"

Ember shook her head. "I don't."

"Goodnight, then," The Collector said, and with a concerned huff, Ember reluctantly left his office. He turned to me again. "I hope you don't have any plans for the evening, Chase. I need you to come with me."

CHAPTER FIVE

THAT NIGHT WAS the first trip I'd taken with The Collector. In fact, it was the first conversation we'd had that lasted longer than ten seconds. As soon as Ember left the tent, he simply put on his coat and asked if I was ready to go. "There's something I need you to see," he said.

Analise, who had been silent so long I forgot she was there, immediately protested. "I'm coming with you," she said in a tone that made it seem like she expected The Collector to disagree.

He shook his head. "Not this time. We'll be going along." Analise objected, but The Collector cut her off. "This is something Chase and I must do alone. I don't foresee us encountering any complications. And if we do, I'm more than capable of keeping us safe."

"Will you at least take Luka? I can tell him to keep his distance, but he could keep an eye on things for you."

"Certainly not," The Collector said as he adjusted the sleeves of his jacket. "My goal is to be inconspicuous. I can't very well do that with a surly giant trudging along behind us, now can I?"

Analise didn't give up so easily. "Sir, I think we can reach an understanding if you'll just —"

"That will be all, Analise," The Collector said. She didn't say another word, just nodded, turned sharply, and left the office. He turned back to me. "Are you ready, Chase?"

"I think so," I said, glancing around the empty office. "Am I — am I in trouble?"

"In trouble?"

It was apparent he was going to make me ask the question I dreaded asking. "Are you taking me to drop me off somewhere?"

"I don't understand," he said as he finished off his drink. "Drop you off?"

I felt like some weird bobble-head doll. I couldn't keep still. I kept glancing around the office, doing my best to concentrate on anything but The Collector. "Am I being taken away? Will I be Forsaken?"

The Collector looked at me like I'd just asked him if there was a chance I might spontaneously burst into flames. "Forsaken? Why on earth do you think that would happen?"

"I don't know. Because Ember and I left the grounds? Because we broke the rules? And we almost caused a lot of trouble for you and the circus?"

The Collector smiled. "Almost," he said as he reached over and patted my shoulder. "You're not being Forsaken," he said flatly. "What possible good would that accomplish?" He paused. "Tell me, son, did you learn your lesson today?"

He called me, son. I nodded and for the first time held eye contact. "Yes, I did. I won't ever do anything like that again. I swear."

"Don't swear, Chase," The Collector said as he glanced away. "This world has a sneaky way of tempting us into the very things we choose to swear off." I nodded and The Collector buttoned his coat. "I only want to show you something. Something you need to see. Come along." He tossed me a plain brown jacket which I put on and zipped up.

The Collector had the ability to travel throughout space and time and could take along anyone he wanted. The concept was simple enough although I had no idea how it worked. In a way it was easy. As natural as breathing or waking up. It happened in an instant. As fast as a blink. One minute you were in ancient Greece and the next you were in the UK at the World's Fair in 1914. The circus moved around the world freely at The Collector's command. It was difficult to know how much or how little time the process of moving everyone actually took because it felt like no more than an instant. The circus and its people, would arrive fully intact and tailor made for whatever time period The Collector had delivered us.

"Alright, Chase," The Collector said. "Close your eyes now."

And as quickly as I closed them, I opened them to find us standing in the middle of a full parking lot on a frigid night. It was sleeting, the frozen pellets bounced off of our jackets and collected at our feet to form a thin carpet of ice on the asphalt. "Where are we?" I asked as soon as my eyes had regained focus.

"Welcome to St. Anne's Hospital, Chicago, Illinois, 1975," The Collector said, looking down at me.

"A hospital?" I said. "Is everything okay?"

"Follow me, Chase."

With steps that crunched beneath us, The Collector led us across the parking lot and into the emergency room of St. Anne's. We stepped through the crowded waiting room and up to the counter where a frazzled young nurse was shuffling papers and sorting clip boards.

"Excuse me," The Collector said as he offered the woman an easy smile. She didn't look at him.

"Yes, can I help you?"

"I'm looking for someone. Perhaps you can help me locate him?"

"What's the name?" she said, still not looking up.

"I'm here to see a young boy admitted earlier this evening, Calvin Jackson?"

At the mention of his name, the nurse finally looked up. "And who are you? You don't look like family."

The Collector smiled again. "I'm not family. I'm a friend of the family."

She glanced down at me and then back at The Collector. "Look, this isn't a good time. I'm afraid you'll have to come back once we move him to a room or after the family shows up."

"Please, Miss," The Collector said, resting his hands on the counter. "I am aware of the unfortunate situation. The boy and I only want to check in on him. See him with our own eyes. Then we'll be on our way."

The nurse glanced around her station to make sure no one else was listening. "I can only give you a minute," she said reluctantly. "He's not doing so well, and the police will be here asking questions soon. If you know the situation, then you know how sensitive this is."

"I do. And I promise, we'll only be a moment." He motioned to me. "This is Chase. He's a friend, and it's very important that he sees Calvin. If only briefly. You understand, don't you?"

The young nursed audibly groaned and grabbed a chart. "Come with me," she said. "But I'm only giving you five minutes. Maybe less. If the police or his family shows up, then you have to go."

"I understand," The Collector said.

"I mean it. Five minutes."

The nurse led us through a narrow maze of sterile corridors until she eventually stopped, pulled open a curtain, and ushered us into a small room. On the bed in front of me was a young boy, no more than six or seven who had been battered and bruised worse than anyone I'd ever seen. He was completely wrapped up and looked to be held together with gauze and tape. Surrounding him were tubes and monitors and flashing lights that blinked and buzzed, all working together to keep the young boy alive.

"The clock is ticking," the nurse said as she left, pulling the curtain behind her.

"Go ahead," The Collector said. "Take a look."

I stepped up beside the boy whose face was swollen and blue. One eye was completely hidden by the puffed up skin around it and the other was taped over with a clean dressing. His chest slowly rose and fell with each rattled breath. I remember thinking how painful those injuries must be and how lucky he was to be unconscious. "Who is this?" I asked. "Why are we here?"

The Collector slid a metal chair across the cold tile floor and sat down on the opposite side of the bed. "This is Calvin Jackson and earlier tonight he was nearly beaten to death by his drunken father."

"What? Why?"

"*Why?*" The Collector said. "I seriously doubt there's any good reason to nearly beat a child to death with a baseball bat. But regardless, he did so because Calvin spilled juice on the carpet."

"Is this real? Are you serious?"

"Gravely so," he said.

"But he's just a kid."

"True, but it wasn't simply the spilled juice that set his father off. Apparently Calvin was afraid he'd be in trouble for staining the carpet, so he began to cry. That only further infuriated dear old dad, and he told him to stop or he'd, 'give him something to cry about.' Apparently, Calvin did not stop. Or at least not soon enough for his father's liking."

"So he *beat* him with a *bat*? Because he spilled juice and cried? Was he arrested? Please tell me he was arrested."

The Collector shook his head. "When his father realized he'd hurt Calvin more than he'd intended, he brought him here to the emergency room. He didn't come in, mind you, he simply laid him down at the front door and ran."

"So, he's still out there? Does anyone even know Calvin is here?"

"Well, that brings us to the issue at hand, Chase," The Collector said as he touched Calvin's arm. "The next person who'll walk through that door will be Calvin's mother, Janelle. Janelle is a good enough woman but not a very capable mother. As you'll hear in a moment, she will be terribly distraught and angry but thrilled to find Calvin alive. After a couple of days, Calvin will be released and she'll take him home. Janelle will do an adequate job making sure he is cared for and soon Calvin will make a full recovery."

"That's a good thing, right?"

"It would be," The Collector said. "However, in two weeks from today, Calvin's father will return home and the family will be together once again."

"I don't understand," I said. "What's all this about?"

"Calvin is special. He's a Prime. Echo found out about him through an old news article about how he'd won a science fair for successfully predicting the weather every day for an entire month. It was uncanny. He got everything correct, even right down to the exact temperature it would be each day."

"That's amazing."

"What's more amazing is that Olivia and I don't believe Calvin was predicting the weather. We believe he was controlling it."

My mouth hung open as I stared at the frail boy lying there on that hospital bed. If what The Collector said was true, one day Calvin could protect himself. He could keep anyone from ever hurting him again. If his dad ever tried to beat him, he could just zap him with lightning if he wanted. He could control his world. His life. He could keep himself safe. But he was just a kid, and he probably didn't even know he had an ability.

"Here's the bottom line," The Collector said. "If Calvin's mother takes him home tonight, his father will return, and in a few months from now he'll accidentally kill Calvin in another drunken fit of rage. If memory serves me, it will be because Calvin wet the bed."

It shouldn't have taken as long as it did, but it finally dawned on me what The Collector was proposing. "So, you're here because he has an ability. You're here to collect him."

"That's partially correct," The Collector said. "But I also brought you along so I could hear your thoughts on the matter. I need you to understand what it is we do at the circus. It's not just about putting on a show, it's about changing lives." He paused. "There's a question I wrestle with for each and every person I collect. Is it cruel for me to take Calvin away from his family, his mother, and his friends in order to save his life? Or is it better for me to step aside and allow fate to control the matter? Should Calvin's life and death be left to the way it naturally happened? Should I intervene? Is it my obligation? Should I save him? Should *we* save him?"

I'd never thought much about the collecting process before that night. I knew my story, but not many circus members talked about their collection. Ember never would. "His mother, Janelle," I said, "is she a kind woman?"

"Would that change your opinion?"

"I don't know. Maybe not. But I'd still like to know."

"Calvin's mother works nearly sixty hours a week to keep the heat running and food on the table. She does love Calvin, but unfortunately Janelle is a product of the world she's grown up knowing. It's not entirely her fault, but the truth is she is incapable of being the sort of mother a young boy needs. Or deserves." There was an emptiness left hanging in the room after those words. It was something about the way The Collector said them. Such grim truth communicated in such an easy manner. No emotion; no compassion. Just facts. I wondered if anyone had ever spoken in such a way about me or my parents. However, there wasn't much time to ponder such things because the silence was suddenly interrupted. A ruckus erupted in the hallway, accompanied by the loud cries of a very upset woman. She was practically screaming, marching through the halls, looking for her boy. Calvin. "You need to decide quickly, Chase. I'm leaving this one up to you. Do we take him now and help him become part of a new family? Or do we leave him here?"

"Why is this up to me? Why is this my decision?"

"Because I need you to understand how this works. I need you to know how seriously I take the practice of uprooting a person's life. Even if it is for their own good. I need you to make this decision. I need you to feel the weight of it. The responsibility."

The nurses just outside the curtain were trying in vain to calm the woman. But despite their best efforts, Calvin's mother only grew louder and demanded to be let in. Words ultimately turned into pushing and a scuffle broke out just on the other side of the curtain. The Collector stood up. "Tell me now, Chase."

For a moment I watched it all play out in my mind. A frightened young boy being pulled out of his bed and beaten to death. His mother crying. His drunk father shocked by his own actions. Calvin's funeral. His life snuffed out through a senseless act. An avoidable act.

"We take him," I said. The curtain was suddenly thrown open, and in that same instant we were gone.

I opened my eyes and was once again in The Collectors office. "Good work tonight, Chase," he said with a grin. He removed his coat and hung it on the rack.

"Where's Calvin?"

"Calvin is in the infirmary. I've made sure he'll get the care he needs. I expect a full recovery."

"Can I see him?"

"Of course," he said. "But for now, I think it would be best if you turn in for the night. As soon as Calvin is ready for visitors, I'll let you know." I nodded and turned to leave when The Collector called out to me again. "For what it's worth, I agree with the decision you made. I would have done the same."

"Thank you."

CHAPTER SIX

"SOMETHING IS WEIRD about all of this," Ember said.

"Well, yeah," I answered, wide-eyed. "I got to collect someone last night. That's about as weird as it gets. Think about that. *I* collected someone. He let me make the decision. I just hope I did the right thing."

Ember shook her head; her face was twisted up. "No, I'm not talking about that. I mean this whole thing is off." She made a point to look into my eyes in that intense way only Ember could. Like she had the ability to will you into listening to her whether you wanted to or not. "Hear me out. We left the grounds yesterday. We *left the grounds,* we had the police called on us, and we got caught. Do you understand how big of a deal that is?"

"I know it's a big deal. The Collector does too. That's why he asked me if I learned anything from —"

"No, Chase," Ember cut in. "We left the grounds, got caught, and *nothing* happened to either of us. That doesn't sound strange to you? We didn't get Forsaken. We didn't get sent to the hole. We didn't even get yelled at. Instead, you got a field trip and I got sent to bed. That's not normal.

Something is off. And, why would he send me away to talk to you in private? He didn't even threaten me not to do it again."

"I don't know what he's thinking. Maybe you're reading too much into this," I offered. "The Collector asked me if I learned my lesson, and I said yes. He's giving us another chance. He's being nice. We should be happy about it."

"I hope you're right," Ember said quietly.

I nodded. "I think I am. Look, if he wanted to, he could have gotten rid of us last night. He could have just said the word and...poof, we'd be gone. But he didn't. He wants us here, Ember. I think he likes us."

"You always want people to like you."

"What does that mean? No, I don't."

"Oh please, Chase," Ember said, rolling her eyes. "You care way too much about what people think of you."

"That's not true."

"Then why didn't you tell The Collector your girl-friend's name?"

"Just stop," I said. Anytime she wanted to upset me, Ember would call Sophia my girlfriend. And just to sprinkle a bit of insult on top, she also loved to call me obsessed, delusional, or stalker. "She's not my girlfriend."

"Why didn't you tell him her name? He asked you who it was you left the circus to see. You had a chance to tell him — you almost did. But then you stopped yourself. Why?"

"What? I — I didn't — it wasn't like that."

Ember latched on like a bulldog. "Just answer the question. Why didn't you say her name? So-phi-a...it's not that hard to say."

"I don't know," I said, raising my voice. "I guess I just — I don't know."

"You were embarrassed."

She was right. And I hated that she was right. "I wasn't embarrassed. I don't have anything to be embarrassed about. I said she's my friend. And she is."

Ember raised an eyebrow, a smug grin on her face. "Yeah. Okay."

I was about to tell Ember something about minding her own business when I was interrupted by one the the guards who'd stepped into my tent. "Chase? Ember? I have a message for you," the young man said. He passed me a plain brown envelope. "This is from The Collector." Then, he simply nodded and left.

Ember and I both glared at the envelope. "Well, I guess we'll see who's right about everything," Ember said. "For the record, I hope it's you."

I quickly tore open the envelope and pulled out a small piece of paper. It was a handwritten note. I read it aloud, "Chase and Ember, I hope you understand how seriously we take it when members of the circus leave the grounds without permission. Your personal safety and the safety of the circus as a whole depends on all of us adhering the rules."

"So far, this doesn't sound too good," Ember said.

I continued reading. "I hope you realize that I care for you both, but it is my responsibility to maintain order within this family. So, please consider this your one and only warning, and help me keep your brothers and sisters safe. To show that I trust you will do as I ask, I have included a gift. If you look inside the envelope, you'll find a day pass and twenty dollars. The pass will allow you to leave the grounds today. Show it to the guard at the gate and he will allow you to pass without issue. The money is so you can purchase the lattes you both enjoy so much. Go, have fun, and be safe." I glanced up at Ember to find she shared my shock and confusion. "It's signed, 'The Collector.'"

"Is leaving the circus a thing?" Ember said. "Like, is that legal? We can do that?"

"I guess so," I said, holding up the pass.

Just then, Echo came barging into the tent, again accidentally bumping into Ember who gritted her teeth to keep from saying something she shouldn't. "Sorry," Echo said, out of breath. "Something happened and I thought you should know."

"For once," Ember said under her breath.

"What is it, Echo?" I said. "What's wrong?"

"It's Setu," Echo said. "He's in the hole. He's in there because he helped you. I - I promise, I didn't tell anyone. But they found out."

Setu wasn't allowed to have visitors. No one in the hole was, but Setu was our friend and we had to check on him. Somehow Ember knew when the guard would come and go, and she was confident we'd have a few moments to talk to Setu when he left to make his rounds.

"Setu?" I whispered as we dropped to our knees beside the hole. "Are you there?"

"I am here," Setu answered weakly. It was so dark in the

hole we couldn't see him. I only caught a few glints of light reflecting off of his eyes as he stared up at us. "You shouldn't be here. If you get caught speaking to me, you'll find yourselves right next to me."

"I'm here too," Ember said. "We had to come tell you we're sorry."

"Yeah, we never meant to get you in trouble," I added. And we never wanted you to end up in the hole."

"Thank you for saying that, but the decision to help you was my own," Setu answered. "No one forced me to do so, and I take responsibility for my own actions."

"Is there anything you need?" I asked. "Can we do anything for you."

"No," Setu said. "Just be careful and make sure you don't end up the same."

"Do you know how long you'll be here?" I said. "Were you told how many days?"

Setu paused for what seemed too long. "I was told I will be here until The Collector decides my fate."

"Decides your fate?" Ember said. "What does that mean?"

"It means he hasn't decided whether or not I'll be allowed to remain a part the circus."

Though Setu's voice was hesitant and unsteady, his words hit me like a tidal wave of regret. I had caused his trouble. I asked Setu to help us sneak away from the grounds. I didn't stop Ember from attacking the man who called the police. It was my fault. "Setu," I said, my voice cracking. "You don't really think he'd make you a Forsaken, do you?"

"It is possible," Setu said dryly. "The Collector may do as he wishes. He told me I'd know within two days."

"Setu, I - I'm sorry," I said, even though I'd already told him that. I didn't think it was possible to say those words enough to make up for what happened.

"Me too," Ember added. Her voice was shaking as well. "If I would have just walked away from that guy, then none of this would have —"

"You can't know that for certain," Setu said. "But, since I know you believe it, I forgive you. Both of you. If you want to repay me, then please don't leave the grounds again."

"Setu," I began, "The Collector gave us passes to leave today. He said it was a gift and told us never to leave without permission again. Do you think it's okay? Should we?"

"If you have permission, you should go," Setu said. "But make the most of your time, Chase. It could very well be the last chance you'll ever have."

"What do you mean? Make the most of it?"

"The girl," Setu said. "What is her name?"

I glanced at Ember who shrugged and looked away. "Her name is Sophia," I said.

"Sophia," he repeated. "A lovely name. And you care for this girl?"

"Yes," I said. "She's my friend."

"I had a girl I cared for once," Setu said. His voice seemed to float up from that pit and into the sky above, sounding as if, for that moment, he was somewhere else. In a different time. A different life.

"Did you?" I asked. I never thought of Setu as a boyfriend or husband, or anything other than...Setu. "What was her name?"

I could see him blinking, and when he spoke it felt like

he was there with her, looking into her eyes. "Her name was Maya, and she was as lovely as a dream."

"How old were you?" I asked. "When you last saw her?"

Setu smiled; I could see his teeth shine. "I was about your age when my father told me about Maya. I barely knew her, but I had noticed her many times. She was beautiful. Father told me she was to be my wife soon, and I couldn't have been happier. Of course, as soon as I found out, I had to know her thoughts on the betrothal. So, she and I began to sneak away to meet. It wasn't permitted for a young man and woman to be alone before marriage. And since we didn't want to take the chance of being caught alone, we'd meet in crowded areas such as the market, standing just close enough to speak, but not so close as to cause suspicion."

"So, you were arranged to be married?" I said. "I don't think most people would like that."

"They would if they were marrying Maya," Setu said. "Although, sadly, it never came to be." He paused. "I was still a teenager when The Collector came for me. I was walking home from one of my visits with Maya when suddenly he was walking alongside me. He explained who he was and why he was there — that he was taking me to be a part of a wonderful circus. A new family. I couldn't bear the thought of leaving just days before Maya and I were to be married, so I ran."

"Wait, you didn't choose to be here? You didn't want to be part of the circus?"

"Not everyone who comes here does so willingly."

"Where did you run?" I said. "How long did it take him to catch you?"

"I ran to find Maya," Setu said. "So we could leave together. I thought I could hide us both, but The Collector and Analise were already waiting at her door when I arrived. I pushed past them and into the house where I found Maya preparing dinner. My ability was no secret to me, but I had yet to share my gift with Maya. I was afraid she'd believe me evil or strange. But, I didn't care about that in the moment. My only concern was transporting us to somewhere we could hide. Somewhere we'd be safe. When I took hold of Maya, I realized my abilities had failed me. They were stripped by Analise. I begged, cried, tried to appeal to The Collector, but he —" Setu suddenly went silent. "I have said too much as it is. I should stop now."

"What happened to Maya? Were you able to see her again?"

"It's been twelve years," Setu said. "Twelve years have passed since The Collector came to my village. It was the last time I saw Maya or my family."

"That's terrible. I'm sorry, Setu."

For a moment there was silence, with only the gentle rustling of wind through the trees and the faint chirping of birds in the distance. "Take this opportunity, Chase. Go to the girl. Tell her how you feel. Leave nothing unsaid."

I wasn't sure how to respond to what he'd said, so I simply grunted something that sounded like, "okay."

"And, Ember?" Setu said.

"Yes, I'm here," she said. It was the first thing she'd said since we first got there, and there was a slight edge to her voice.

"You need to support Chase. Go with him. Help him. This is important. It's important for both of you."

"I'll help him," Ember said, her voice void of emotion. Then, something caught her attention. "We need to go. The guard is coming."

"We're leaving now, Setu," I said. "But, just hold on. We'll find a way to help you."

"Don't worry about me," Setu said. "Take care of yourselves. Take care of one other."

❧

"How long is this going to take, Chase?" Ember said sharply as she stood there with her arms crossed. We'd used our pass without incident. The guard nodded and let us walk right through the front gate. We made our way back to Sophia's, and, for the second time in as many days, we were standing on the street in front of her house. "Just go up to the door and knock. When she answers, tell her you love her and let's go."

"Why are you being so rude?"

"I'm not being rude. I just don't like spending what may be my last day out of the circus listening to you profess your love to some girl."

"I'm not here to profess my love," I snapped. "I'm just here to say hello to a friend. And stop calling her *some girl*. You know her name is Sophia."

"Sorry. I forgot," Ember said with a shrug as she turned her back on me.

"Oh, I'm sure you did. What is wrong with you anyway? If you have something to say to me, then just say it."

Ember whipped her head around and glared at me like a fight to the death wasn't out of the question. "Trust me, you don't want to hear what I have to say."

I'd seen Ember get like that before, intense and angry. Usually it didn't turn out well, but I wasn't about to back down on the subject. "I want you to say whatever you want to say," I said, throwing my arms up. "I'm tired of you snapping at me every time I mention Sophia. If you have something to tell me, I want to hear it. So, say it."

I could practically see Ember's anger bubbling just beneath the surface. Boiling up behind her eyes. But whatever tirade was swelling inside of her, she somehow managed to force it back down before it boiled over. "I don't care anymore. It doesn't matter what I think anyway. Do whatever you want, Chase," she said as she walked away. "You can come find me at the coffee shop when you're done embarrassing yourself." Ember stomped off and I made my way up the stone pathway to the front door as I rolled my eyes. Ember was a good friend. One that never made you guess where she stood on practically any subject. But her jealousy sometimes got the best of her.

With each step, my anxiety grew. As much as I'd rehearsed that moment over and over in my mind, the truth was, I had no idea what I would say when Sophia was standing in front of me. It had been so long since we'd talked. Would she still remember me? Would she even know my name? Did she ever think about me like I thought about her? But mostly

I wondered if I was about to make a fool of myself. Like Ember said I would.

When I reached out for the front door, I noticed my hands were shaking. I tried to calm myself by repeating the words in my head. *Don't be stupid. She's just a girl. A friend. She'll probably be happy to see you.* Of course, I had no way of knowing whether or not that was true. But I did know, that afternoon might be the only chance I'd ever have to talk to her again. Like Setu said, I couldn't waste the opportunity. So, I closed my eyes, took a deep breath, reached out, and pressed the doorbell. Over the thudding of my own heart, I could hear noise coming from inside. Something like bare feet running across a hardwood floor. A small dog barked and a girl called out, "I'll get it." Before I even had a chance to properly panic, the door swung open and Sophia was standing there looking at me.

There were three things I instantly decided in that moment. First, Sophia had to be the prettiest girl I'd ever seen. Even more so than I remembered. She was pretty in the way that made it seem like she wasn't trying to be. Her hair was longer than I remembered, dark brown hair that matched her eyes and framed her face in a perfectly natural way. And she was smiling. The smile I remembered. It was the type of smile that made you believe she was genuinely happy to see you. Second, my legs turned to jelly and I thought I might pass out right there in front of her. I was surprised by that. There were some things I expected. Butterflies — yes. Nausea — sure. But literally passing out? I didn't see that coming. And lastly, in that moment, I could no longer deny that I was a liar. I had been lying for a long time. For two years I had talked about Sophia, mostly to Ember. I'd told her about every conversation we'd had, every class we'd taken together, and had gone into great detail describing every school event or party we'd shared. Through it all, I consistently tried to convince Ember that I didn't like Sophia in a *girlfriend* kind of way. I had tried to convince myself as well. And when I did talk about Sophia, I always used the same word…friend. But that afternoon, the truth reached out and slapped me in the face as soon as she opened the door. I didn't think of Sophia as a friend. I loved her.

CHAPTER SEVEN

I WAS TWELVE years old when I met Sophia. I had just started a new school and the family with which I'd been placed, thought it would be good for me to go to a class party. They said it would help me fit in. To meet new people. I'd never been to a class party. I'd never been to a party of any type. But there I was, dressed in khakis and a button up shirt, holding a present wrapped in shiny pink paper with a white bow. "Well, come on inside," Mrs. Pace said in her sing-song voice. "Don't you look so nice." Mrs. Pace was Madison's mom and room parent for my class. She could typically be seen hugging anyone who wandered to close to her and smiling wildly through bright red lipstick.

I immediately felt out of place. Music was playing, kids were squealing and laughing, and moms and dads were gathered in the kitchen sipping coffee and swapping stories about homework struggles. I suppose it could have been fun if I had known any of the kids in my class. I'd only been in my new home for two weeks and it just so happened that Madison's birthday fell within that time frame. Everyone in the class was invited and being the new kid apparently didn't excuse me.

I added my gift to the other pink presents that practically spilled off of the gift table as I turned around to a sturdy pat on the back. "Hey, Chase," Victor said with a broad grin. Victor was a kid in my class and one of the only guys who'd made any effort to talk to me. "You want some punch?" he asked as he tried to wipe away his red mustache.

"Hey, Victor," I said. "How long have you been here?"

"Just got here. Right before you," he said. I found that interesting seeing as how his hair was already wet with sweat, his shirt was untucked, and he was halfway through a hot dog.

"Do you know everybody here?" I asked as I nervously scanned the room. There were so many kids there, and I was sure there were several I'd never seen.

"No, but I know most of them," he said. "I've met some people though. You want me to introduce you?" I tried to say no, but Victor was too quick. He started grabbing kids and pulling them up, "Hey do you know, Chase?" he'd ask. "He's new." Startled kid after startled kid was shoved toward me by a gleeful Victor as they all stammered a "hello" and darted away. It was the last thing I wanted. Being the center of attention was something I generally avoided at all costs. For Victor though, it came as naturally as breathing.

After about the fifth forced introduction, I was more than happy to hear Madison's mom announce, "Okay kids, everyone come into the living room and find a seat." I followed the crowd to find a circle of white folding chairs waiting on us. Victor quickly grabbed a seat and motioned for me to take the chair next to him. Everyone was laughing, talking, and generally being happy kids. A room full of loud boys and girls who felt perfectly at ease around one another. I was envious of that. It was a feeling I'd never experienced. "We're going to play a little 'get to know you' game before we open presents," Mrs. Pace continued. She placed a hand on my shoulder. "I thought it would be good for all of us to share a little about ourselves." All eyes turned to me and I wanted to melt and evaporate on the spot. Luckily she started at the opposite side of the circle. "We'll start with the birthday girl, Madison," she cheered through the return of her sing-song voice. "Tell everyone your name and one thing about you that no one knows."

Madison thought hard for a moment as her friends whispered into her ear and giggled. "Well…" she said finally, "My name is Madison."

The group laughed and in unison echoed back, "Hi, Madison."

"And something no one knows about me is…I snore really loud when I sleep." Everyone laughed as if Madison had just said the funniest thing they'd ever heard. I didn't laugh. Not because I didn't want to, but because it wasn't very funny to me. Laughter never came easily to me. In fact, not many emotions did. Yet another thing I envied.

The girl next to Madison was Julia, and she broke her arm when she fell out of her bunk bed in third grade. Garrett was next. He wanted to be a professional football player one day. I don't think anyone considered that, 'something they didn't know.' Kid after kid introduced themselves and told some random fact to the rest of us. Some were funny, like the kid who claimed he punched the mall Santa in the face when he was three, or the girl who said she didn't know how to ride a bike. But others were a little more serious. One girl said both of her grandparents died last year, and another girl, named Celia, said her dog ran away three weeks ago. We made our way around the circle quickly, and soon it was Victor's turn. He proudly announced his name to the group followed up with a long story about how he went on vacation to the beach and almost drowned. Only Victor could have told a story about nearly drowning that would make everyone laugh.

Then, it was my turn. My first attempt at speaking resulted in coughing and having to clear my throat several times just to make a sound come out. "My name is Chase," I finally managed to say.

Everyone followed with a hearty, "Hi, Chase."

Then it was time for my fact, and although I'd had plenty of time to think, I had no idea what to say. The only thing that came to mind was that my mom and dad died before I was old enough to remember them, but I wasn't about to say that. I had also lived in several foster homes, but that wasn't something I wanted anyone to know, much less a room full of twelve-year-olds. I had to say something. The seconds were ticking away and I was beginning to panic.

"It's okay, dear," Mrs. Pace said. "Take your time. Just say the first thing that comes to your mind."

So I did. "Like I said, my name is Chase and…I haven't ever cried."

There wasn't much of a response. A couple of kids whispered to each another, a few seemed shocked, and some looked at me like they didn't believe me. Predictably, Victor was the first to speak. "No way. How is that possible? You mean you've never cried? *Never?* Like not even once?"

It was the truth. I couldn't remember ever crying. I had been hurt and I had been sad, but not once had I ever cried. Not that I could recall. "I haven't," I said as the room went silent. "It just hasn't ever happened."

It felt like a month went by, sitting there while everyone looked at me like I was the main attraction at a freak show. The quietness lingered until it was nearly unbearable before a single voice cut through the room. The quiet voice of a girl. "It's okay, Chase," she said. "Not everyone cries, and some people cry too much." Everyone turned their attention to her. Her hands were resting on her lap in a way that made her seem perfectly comfortable, and she looked at me with a kind smile. A pretty girl in a pale blue dress with long brown hair and soft eyes to match. Sophia.

It took a moment for my mouth to begin working, but after a couple of tries, I finally managed to force out a few words. "Sophia? You're Sophia, right?" *Of course she's Sophia you idiot.* "Do you remember me?"

I could see the wheels turning in her mind. She was chewing on her lip and her brow was wrinkled. Apparently she had some memory of me, but her puzzled look made it clear she hadn't quite worked it out. She wasn't giving up though. Then, as my doubts were about to overtake me, the smile I'd missed so much slowly stretched across Sophia's face. Her eyes lit up and she rose up on her tiptoes. "Chase?" she said softly. Then louder. "Chase, is that really you?"

"It is," I said, unable to contain the smile of my own.

To my surprise, Sophia reached out with both arms, pulled me in close, and hugged me in a way that made me wish she'd never let go. "I've missed you. Where have you been?" she said as she pulled away. "It's like you were here one day, and then you just…disappeared."

Disappeared. I wanted to answer her truthfully, but I wasn't exactly sure what to say. Somehow the idea of telling her, *I was collected by a circus full of people with special powers that moves throughout space and time,* didn't seem appropriate. "Yeah, I—I moved," I said. Which was sort of true.

Before the next question had the chance to leave Sophia's lips, her mom was at the door to welcome me as well. She and Sophia looked alike. They had the same gentle eyes. Even though I'd never met her before that day, her mom acted like she'd known me for years. It made me wonder if Sophia had mentioned me before. If she'd ever told her mom about a kid named Chase that she was friends with once. However, I hardly had time to think about anything because I was quickly swept into their home, ushered into the living room, seated on a sofa, and handed a glass of lemonade. All of that before I could even process the fact that I was actually in Sophia's home — the home I'd stood out on the street and stared at for hours. Which, even thinking of it like that, made me feel like a creep. But, in that moment, I didn't care. It felt like being in the middle of a recurring dream, one I was suddenly given the chance to step inside of and wander around. My only regret was that I hadn't done it sooner.

Sophia climbed into the chair next to the sofa and settled in like she was ready for a long talk. "So, what have you been doing for the last two years?" she said as she pulled her hair out of her face. There was something about the way she asked the question that was different. Ember and I talked all of the time about all sorts of things, but when Sophia spoke to me, it didn't feel the same. When Sophia asked what I'd been doing, I felt like she truly wanted to know. Like it wasn't just talk; she actually cared about how I was. It was nice, but I wasn't equipped to handle it well. Making friends had never been easy for me, and it usually took a while for me to open up. The fact that it came so easily to Sophia made me anxious. I felt flattered, important, and awkward all at the same time, mostly because I wasn't sure why she cared in the first place. It was strange for me to feel cared about by someone I hardly knew.

I took a sip of my lemonade to gather my thoughts, angry at myself that I hadn't thought of a good answer to that question before showing up. "I've been traveling," I said as I set my glass on the coaster. "I'm with a circus."

"A circus?" she said raising her eyebrows. "How in the world did you end up in a circus?"

"It's a long story," I said. "But it's fun. Ever since I got collected, I've been able to travel and meet really cool people."

"Collected?" Sophia said.

"Well, I— I meant to say, not collected, but recruited."

Sophia's mom must have been listening from the other room. She walked in carrying a plate of cookies. "Well, that certainly sounds exciting. Is that the circus that's in town now? I was thinking about all of us going. I've heard great things about it."

"Yeah, we just opened last night, so we'll be here for at least a few days. We had a big crowd yesterday."

"Oh, I *have* heard about that," Sophia said. "Is there a girl that does something with fire? Some of my friends were there last night and they were telling me how awesome it was."

"Yeah, that's us," I said. "You should come. We have a lot of acts."

"Like what?" Sophia said as she inched a bit closer.

"Well, we have a knife thrower named Julius. He hangs from his feet while he spins and throws knives at moving targets. He's pretty amazing."

Sophia's mom sat down next to me. "What else?"

"Umm…there's a lady named Gladys who bends metal plates. Bars too. She gets audience members to come up and challenge her. It's always funny to watch the big guys try to outdo her. They can't even come close. Some of them say it's rigged, but they're just embarrassed."

"Where do you find all these people?" Sophia asked.

"Like I said, we travel a lot," I answered carefully. "All over the world. And if you look hard enough, you can always find people who can do amazing things."

"What about you?" Sophia said. "Are you in an act? Do you do anything…amazing?"

"If you consider picking up trash amazing, then yes," I said, doing my best to act like that fact didn't bother me. "I still don't know where I'll end up. I guess you could say I'm starting at the bottom. Hopefully something will change soon."

Sophia smiled. "I'm sure you'll do something great."

"Yeah, I hope so."

Sophia's mom got up and crossed the living room to a large trophy case. "Have you seen these, Chase?" she said.

"Please don't, Mom," Sophia said with a groan.

I went over to look into the case which was full, top to bottom, with shiny gold trophies, ribbons of all different colors, and embossed medals. "What is this?" I said, leaning in to get a better look. "Sophia, are these yours?"

Sophia sighed and her mom interjected. "Yes, they are hers, and she should be proud of them. Shes runs. And she's fast."

Sophia attempted to speak, "I'm okay. Mom just thinks —"

"She's really fast," her mom said. "Not only did she make the varsity track team as a freshman, she also set school records in four different events."

I glanced over at Sophia; her head was down and she had turned a slight shade of red. "Okay, Mom, I'm sure Chase doesn't care anything about that. Thanks though."

"I think it's impressive," I said.

That seemed to please Sophia's mom. "Well, if that circus of yours is looking for someone fast, you tell them to come talk to us," she said with a smirk.

"I will," I said with a laugh. I glanced at the clock on the wall and realized I'd been there much longer than I thought. "I really need to get going now. They're expecting me back at the circus." And Ember was expecting me for coffee. Unfortunately, it didn't look like I was going to make it to that coffee date.

"It was so good seeing you, Chase," Sophia's mom said as she placed a hand on my shoulder. "Sophia, walk Chase out, okay?"

"Alright, Mom," Sophia said as we moved toward the foyer.

Sophia had just opened the door when her mom called out from the living room, "Come back and see us next time you're in town."

As we stepped outside and Sophia closed the door behind us, the harsh reality hit me. I wouldn't be coming back to see them. I wouldn't be sitting in their living room drinking lemonade and talking about track meets. The truth was, I would never see Sophia again. There was no way The Collector would give me another chance to leave the circus. That day was a one-time pass. A gift, but a warning. I somehow had to accept that standing there in front of her house would be the last time Sophia and I would ever talk. I could practically hear Setu's words rising up out of that hole in the ground where he was hidden away. *Take this opportunity, Chase. Go to the girl. Tell her how you feel. Leave nothing unsaid.*

Leave nothing unsaid. "Sophia?" I said as my heart began to race. "I wanted to thank you."

"Thank me?" She smiled nervously. "Thank me for what?"

"Do you remember when I first came to school? When we first met each other?"

She tilted her head in thought. "I think so. Was it…at Madison Pace's birthday party?"

"Yeah that was it." I paused. "That party — that was a tough time for me. I had just been put with a new family in a new home and was starting a new school. A lot of the kids there weren't very nice."

"I remember," she said with a somber smile.

"But you weren't like that. You were my friend. When everyone else decided that I was some weirdo they weren't going to talk to, you *kept* being my friend. You talked to me. You hung out with me. You sat with me at lunch."

"They were just a bunch of jerks," she said flatly. "You didn't deserve to be treated like that. I'm sorry."

"It's okay. Well, it was okay because of you. And I never thanked you for that. So, before I go, I — I just wanted to let you know that I appreciate what you did for me."

For the second time, Sophia hugged me, and again I wished it didn't have to end. "Take care of yourself, Chase," she said. "Be careful while you're out there traveling the world."

"I will. And you keep running. And winning."

We said our goodbyes and I walked away feeling a mixture of sadness and peace. I wasn't sure if I'd accomplished what Setu had advised — to leave nothing unsaid. But I felt like I'd said enough. I only hoped that I'd be able to move on and not spend every day thinking about Sophia or wishing I could be with her.

CHAPTER EIGHT

EMBER WAS WAITING for me outside of Sophia's. She was pacing the street in front of the house, and even from a distance I could see the impatience in her rigid steps. I knew she was upset that I'd stayed so long. That I hadn't met her at the coffee shop like we'd agreed. I hoped she would understand. I was wrong.

"You never showed," she said as I walked up. "You told me you would meet me, and you never showed up. I sat there like some sad idiot drinking coffee alone." Her words were sharp. Stabbing. Like a snake bite.

"Ember, I'm sorry. We started talking and —"

"Don't tell me you're sorry," she snapped. "You're not sorry. You are far from sorry. In fact, you finally got what you've always wanted." She jabbed a finger toward Sophia's house. "You got to hang out in there and talk about the good old days with the girl you love."

"It wasn't like that."

"Oh, it wasn't?" Ember said feigning sincerity. "Then please tell me how it was. I've been waiting so long to hear about it."

I needed the conversation to end as quickly as possible,

before something was said we'd both regret. "Look, I knew this would be —" I started; then stopped. I had to choose my words carefully. "Today was the one and only chance I'll ever have to talk to Sophia. I had to make sure I told her everything I needed to say. Like Setu said I should."

"And what was that? What did you need to say that was so important it took you two years to say it?" Ember was breathing heavily and her eyes were glassy. If I hadn't known better, I'd have thought she was going to cry. Which was something I'd never seen before. I assumed she and I were alike in that way.

"I needed to thank her," I said. "That's all." I was going to leave it at that, but Ember just stood there with her eyebrows raised, waiting for more. "She was my friend when she didn't have to be. When no one else was. She…looked out for me."

Ember nodded. "Oh, so kind of like I did when you first came to the circus, right? And every day since?"

"Yes. Like that."

She stood there quietly reeling, hands fidgeting. There was a hateful look on her face, like she was searching for just the right words that would hurt the most. And in that moment of unbearable silence, the mark on our necks tingled. My hand instinctively rose to my mark, but Ember seemed to ignore it completely. "That's all just great," she said. "Very kind of you. So maybe if you ever leave the circus, you can come back one day and thank me too. Like in a couple of years."

"Ember, it doesn't matter anymore. It's not like I'll ever see her again."

"The fact that you think it doesn't matter shows me just how clueless you are."

"What do you want from me?" I said, raising my voice. I could feel the heat rising in my chest. "Seriously, what do you want me to do? What can I say to make this any better?"

Ember narrowed her eyes at me and spoke quietly. "Nothing, Chase. Don't say anything."

"Well, apparently there's something you want to hear, and I'm just not saying it."

"Wrong again," Ember said as she turned to leave. "I don't need anything from you. In fact, don't even talk to me anymore."

"Ember, wait," I said racing toward her.

She turned on me; her eyes flashed with anger and flames. When she spoke it was more like a threat than a statement. "Leave me alone, Chase. I don't want to talk to you now. I don't want to talk to you later. I'm not sure I ever want to talk to you again. Leave me alone. For good." Ember continued her march toward the circus grounds and I followed at a safe distance. A hair-trigger temper was certainly something Ember was known for, and, while I never thought she'd do anything to hurt me, I didn't want to take the chance. She was too powerful to push.

Our hike of silence lasted until we reached the grounds and the guards held the gates open for us. Ember went through ahead of me and wasted no time increasing the distance between us. I was so focused on Ember that I didn't recognize something was wrong. There was a buzz in the air. It was quiet, and the usual bustle of activity was nonexistent. People were gathered in small groups speaking in hushed tones. Their eyes followed Ember and me as we entered and moved through the grounds. Something was definitely off.

I didn't have to wonder very long. Almost as quickly as I had noticed the strange feeling, Echo again came racing up to me with a look of dread on his face. "Chase I — I need to tell you — I need to tell you something. Ember too. Where is she?"

"What's wrong?"

"Both of you. I —I need to tell you both."

"She's not here. Don't worry about it. Tell me what's wrong, Echo. What happened?"

"It's Setu," Echo replied, trying to catch his breath. "While you were gone, The Collector — he sent him away."

"What are you talking about, Echo?" I said. "What do you mean he sent him away?"

"I mean there was a meeting while you were gone. The Collector called all of us together. He said that Setu was guilty of treason for helping you sneak out yesterday. He said that treason was the worst crime any member of the circus could commit."

"What happened?" I said. My heart was racing and I wasn't sure I wanted to know. "Where is Setu now? Is he still in the hole?"

"No," Echo said, trying to catch his breath. "He — he's gone."

"Gone? What do you mean he's gone?"

Echo glared at me like he'd just witnessed a horrible accident. "The Collector sent him away. He's been Forsaken."

"Please tell me that isn't true," I said.

"It is," Echo said with a stutter. "It's true. He sent him away earlier. We all saw it happen."

I couldn't wait for Echo to explain anything more. Instead, I took off toward The Collector's tent. I didn't know if he would let me in or not, but I had to find out what happened. My legs were tired and I was gasping for breath by the time I reached his tent. There were guards in front but I ran right by them as they yelled and chased after me. With no regard for the consequences, I raced into The Collector's office to find him quietly sitting at his desk, using a feathered quill to craft a letter.

"I need to talk to you," I blurted out. He never looked up. "I said, I need to talk to you," I said louder. The two guards entered immediately and one of them grabbed me in a headlock.

"Let him go," The Collector said. He continued writing.

Reluctantly, the man released me. "Our apologies, sir," one of them said. "He ran right past us."

The Collector finally looked up. "We'll discuss that later. For now, the boy can stay." The guards left and The Collector motioned for me to sit down in the chair in front of his desk. As I took my seat, the realization of what I'd just done began to sink in. No one barges into The Collector's office. No one rushes past our guards. No one demands a meeting. No one who wants to remain a part of the circus anyway.

"Sir, I'm sorry I —" I began, but The Collector held a hand up to silence me.

He gently placed the letter he was working on in the desk drawer and put his pen and jar of ink away. He took a sip of the drink on his desk, sat back, and looked at me. "I assume you are here because of Setu."

"Yes, sir."

"And I assume you've barged into my quarters in such a hawkish manner because you've heard what happened and you disagree with my decision. Is that correct?"

"I heard Setu was Forsaken, but I don't know if it's true. I want to find out. And if it is true, I want to know why."

"Setu…did you consider him a friend?"

"Yes, I did," I said. "I've known Setu since I came here."

"Tell me, Chase," The Collector said, "do you know how long Setu has been with the circus?"

"I'm not sure. A few years?"

"Thirteen years," he said. "The last ten of those, he served as a guard. Being a guard in this circus is a critical role with little room for error. Do you understand that?"

"Yes, I do, but I don't know why —"

"I don't think you do understand," The Collector cut in. "Being a guard is not simply manning the gates and working security during the shows. There are threats out there. Serious threats that would love to tear down this family we've built. Evil men and women intent on destroying people like us. Like you. It is my job to protect us from those threats, and one means by which I do so is by training and utilizing our guards."

"But Setu was good at his job. He cared about us. He kept us safe."

"Setu could not be trusted," The Collector said with a firm tone. "He jeopardized the safety of this circus when he assisted you in leaving the grounds. He also put your life and Ember's in danger. He knew full well what the penalty would be for such actions when he did so."

"So, where did you send him?" I knew when I asked the question that he wouldn't answer.

"You know how being Forsaken works, Chase."

I did know. And it was a terrifying thought. Anytime a member of the circus committed an act The Collector considered treasonous or one that put the circus in danger, that person would become Forsaken. It was a banishment. Setu was now Forsaken. The Collector sent him away. Dropped him off in some random time and place in history where he knew no one. Cut off from friends, from family. He'd have no one. And that is where Setu would spend the rest of his life. Lost. Forgotten.

"But why? Why didn't you let us at least say goodbye?"

The Collector paused for a moment. He was looking right at me, but he seemed like he was somewhere else. Adrift in his own thoughts. "Saying goodbyes doesn't change the fact that someone is gone. Setu was here. Now he is not. I spared you from seeing your friend experience public humiliation and becoming a Forsaken. There's nothing you could have said or done to prevent it."

"So, letting us leave today was just to get us out of the way? So we wouldn't cause trouble or make a scene?"

"Watch your tone, Chase," The Collector said as he sat up in his seat. His words were pointed and direct. "Allowing you to leave the grounds today was a show of trust, despite the fact that you have given me no reason to do so. I suggest you consider that carefully before you question my intentions again. Now, you may go."

I wanted to say something. To ask more questions. To challenge him. "Yes, sir," I said as I stood.

The Collector called to me just as I was leaving his office, "Chase, I believe Olivia is waiting for you. It's time for your next session. Head there straight away, please."

As I trudged along on my way to meet Olivia, I couldn't help but think about how much had happened in the last few hours. Ember wasn't talking to me and Setu had become Forsaken. It was terrible. But then there was also the fact that I'd met with Sophia, which was wonderful and terrible all at once. My mind couldn't keep up with everything which made me even more anxious about meeting with Olivia. She constantly pushed me to focus. To have my breakthrough. It was like a clock was ticking in her head, counting down to the moment I wouldn't be allowed to stay with the circus anymore. Until the day I became like Setu.

"How are you, Chase?" Olivia began. "I know this must be a very difficult day for you."

It was odd to hear Olivia asking about my day. She wasn't one for pleasantries or small talk. "I just don't understand," I said. "I don't understand what was so bad that Setu had to be Forsaken. What he did, he did because I asked him to. It should be me who's Forsaken. Not Setu."

Olivia took a deep breath and returned to her usual prickly self. "Choose your words carefully, Chase. Setu made his choice and paid the price for it. You were fortunate. Learn from this and move on. There's nothing to be done now."

"I still don't like it."

Olivia sat down in her usual spot and took a long hard look at me. "Rules are very important to The Collector. He believes order and loyalty should be honored above all else. He trusted Setu. And whether or not you and I agree, he believes Setu betrayed his trust. He acted accordingly."

I didn't even know why I was talking to Olivia about Setu. It may have been because I knew Ember wouldn't talk to me and I needed to get it out. But, it was evident the conversation wouldn't go in any direction I wanted it to. I wanted to be mad. To vent. Olivia wasn't someone I could vent to. "It's fine," I said. "Let's just get started."

"I'm glad to see you're ready to get to work. We have a lot to accomplish."

I took my spot, relaxed, closed my eyes, and in an instant I was somewhere else. As the scene came into focus, I heard Olivia's voice. "Tell me what you see, Chase."

Just like my previous session, things seemed fuzzy and unfocused. I felt arms around me. I was being held. Carried by someone. I was an infant again. We were rushing through a white hallway that had different colored stripes painted on the floor, turning left, then right. Moving quickly. Window-less walls streaked by and my head bobbled as we rushed along. "I think I'm in a hospital," I said to Olivia.

"A hospital? Good," she said. "Focus. Keep going."

After a few moments of zooming through identical cor-ridors, I was facing a door. A hand reached out and slowly pushed it open. The hand of a man. We eased into the room where a woman with dark hair was lying still on the bed. When I saw her my heart beat faster and I kicked my legs. Someone else was in the room. A young man half asleep in a chair beside the bed. As we stepped inside he lifted his head, and at the sight of me, leapt to his feet. "What are you doing with my son?" he cried out. He had no sooner taken a step toward us when the silhouette of a very large figure passed by me and popped the man on the forehead with an opened palm. He fell back into the chair, unconscious.

I still couldn't see clearly. Things were bright and unfocused, blurring with each movement. I heard a voice, one that seemed familiar. The deep voice of the man holding me reverberated through me, and when he spoke, his words were soft and gentle. "Here she is, Chase," he said. The room turned and spun, shapes and faces streaking past. I was placed on the bed next to the woman. The man took hold of my tiny hand and placed it in hers as he continued in his soothing voice. "You know her, don't you?" he said. "It's your mother. Say, hi. Say, hi, Chase."

Another voice cut through the quiet, startling me, and I began to cry. A woman's voice, harsh and demanding. "Gentlemen, you can't be in here. You need to go."

"Certainly," the man said. "We were just stopping by to say hello. We'll be on our way now."

"Thank you," the woman said. "But you should have checked in at the desk first."

"I understand," he said. "My apologies."

I was lifted from the bed, the world whirling around me. The man turned me around, and I was there face to face with him. "We'll be back," he said to me. And as my tiny eyes focused, I found myself staring into a very familiar face. The face of The Collector.

CHAPTER NINE

"WHAT WAS THAT?" I said as I awoke from my trance.

"What do you mean? It was a memory," Olivia replied. She tried to act casual about it, but I could see the nervous energy in the way she stood and began rearranging items on her desk.

"Why was The Collector in my memories?" I said. "I didn't meet The Collector until just two years ago. How is that possible? And why was he carrying me around? Did he know my mom and dad?"

"Chase," Olivia began, "memories are a complicated thing." She stopped fiddling with the things on her desk and took her seat again. "They aren't entirely accurate. Just because you saw The Collector in your memory doesn't mean he was actually there."

"But he *was* there. You saw him too, didn't you?"

"Yes, I saw him. I see exactly what you see." She paused and looked away, shaking her head. It was apparent by the sour look on her face that she didn't want to have the conversation. "The mind is complex. Sometimes things from the past can get mixed up or combined in a way that can be confusing. Yes, The Collector was in your memory, but you know there is no logical reason for him to be there. What you saw was likely nothing more than your mind filling in the gaps for areas where the memories are incomplete. It's quite common. I see it all the time."

"But it seemed so real."

"In a sense it was. Your mind made it real." She paused. "Don't let this upset you. What we need to concentrate on is you discovering your ability."

I released a deflating breath. "I'm beginning to think that doesn't exist either."

"I disagree," Olivia said. "It's there. We'll find it."

"Can I ask a question?" I said hesitantly. "And will you answer honestly?"

Olivia seemed to soften a bit. "Yes, Chase. What is it?"

"What if we don't find my ability? What if it isn't there?"

"I'd rather us not worry about that now. Worrying can only make the process more difficult. We need to concentrate on —"

"I'm already worried," I said. "I just want to know. I need to know. Will I end up like Setu? If we can't figure it out, will I become a Forsaken?"

Olivia pursed her lips and looked aside as if she was running all possible scenarios through her mind. When she finally spoke, she leaned in close to me and spoke just above a whisper, like she was nervous someone might overhear. "I want to be clear when I say, I don't believe you have anything to worry about. The Collector wants you here. He believes in you. But, if I am being honest, I have seen young people become Forsaken when their abilities couldn't be uncovered."

Even though I suspected it was the case, it still felt like

a punch in the gut. The thought of being dropped off in the middle of a strange country in some unknown point in history made me instantly terrified and nauseated. "How long do I have?"

"I can't answer that. I don't know."

"What about the others?" I said. "Those who were Forsaken before me? How long did they get?"

Olivia looked at me like she was about to tell me I had a terminal illness. Compassion mixed with inevitability. "The ones before you, the ones who didn't manifest and were sent away…None of them were here as long as you've been."

"So, I don't have much longer."

Olivia paused and stared at her feet. "We need to increase our efforts."

⌁

It had been two days since Ember and I had talked. Two days of awkward glances, avoiding one another, and me spending a lot of time with Echo. As much as I wanted to talk to her, to make things right, I wasn't sure she wanted the same. The last thing Ember said to me was not to speak to her ever again. While I knew she didn't mean it, I wasn't sure how long she would need her space. I still went to her shows as I normally did, and I waited for her afterward, as usual, but she never showed. Her shows were still great, Ember was still amazing, and there was nothing to imply that anything was bothering her.

So, that night after the circus gates closed, Echo and I sat by the fire having a meaningless conversation about which of the large cats was the most dangerous to humans. Turns out Echo was still undecided, but he was leaning toward the Bengal Tiger. "Hey, Echo," I said, interrupting his rambling on fang sizes and bite pressure. "Can you do research on current and former circus members?"

Echo tilted his head and squinted. "What type of research?"

Echo was skittish, like an overcautious little bird. I had to move slowly. "Things like, when they joined the circus, where they're from, when they manifested, or...," I paused, "if they were Forsaken?"

"If the information exists I could find it, but those files would probably be restricted."

"But if you wanted to, you *could* see them, right? Even if they were restricted?"

"Theoretically, yes," Echo said, blinking. I could feel him tensing up.

"I'm not asking you to do anything," I said casually. "I'm just asking if it's possible."

"Possible, yes. Good for my mental and physical well-being, no," Echo said with a shaky laugh. "But, why? Why would you want that information?"

I knew if I asked enough questions, curiosity would start to get the best of him. "I was just wondering about Setu," I said. "I was wondering if there was any record of where he was sent or when the decision was made."

Echo's eyes grew large. "Oh, that would definitely be restricted."

"I understand. What about me?"

"You?"

"Yeah, do you think there's any record of how long they'll give me to manifest before I'm...you know?"

Echo sat up straight. "You think they'll make you a Forsaken if you don't manifest soon?"

"I've heard it can happen. I just wanted to know for sure."

Echo stared at the fire, blinking rapidly and struggling with whatever thoughts were zooming through his mind. Something nearby caught my eye and I glanced up to see a thin man in a white shirt and green bow tie standing beside one of the tents. He was barely visible in the dim glow of the surrounding fires, but he was close enough that I knew it was the same man I'd seen a few days earlier. That night was the second time I saw the man in the green bow tie. The first time I had played it off as some sort of odd, random thing that my mind tried to make seem important. But that night, I knew there was more to it than just coincidence. He was not a part of the circus. He was not a visitor; we were closed for the night. He was something more. Something dangerous. He was watching me.

"Stay here; I'll be back," I said to Echo as I jumped to my feet and took off in the direction of the stranger. As I raced toward him, the man quickly ducked behind the tent next to him, but I knew there was no real place for him to hide. There was only row after neat row of small, dark tents the kids all called Tent City, but most circus members simply called home. As I ran, the thought hit me that I had no idea what I'd do when I caught up to him. But I had to find out who the man was and what he wanted. I quickly reached the spot where I'd last seen him and began to move tent by tent, alley by alley, searching for him. Checking every area.

Row by row I moved along, scanning each alleyway, right and left, before sprinting to the next.

Empty…Empty…Empty…

Just when I was beginning to lose hope of finding him, the man in the green bow tie stepped out from behind a tent about four rows ahead of me. He looked at me, startled, then turned and ran. I chased after him, doing my best to keep him in my sights. At the end of the row he turned left heading toward the open area of the main grounds. I only lost sight of him for a second, but when I rounded the corner, he was gone. Still, I continued to run because I hoped I'd see him as soon as I reached the clearing. I exited the Tent City into the main grounds and nearly barreled right into someone. I managed to skid to a halt, nearly tripping over my own feet, before colliding with a girl who happened to be passing by. Ember.

"Look out!" she cried out as she instinctively pushed me away. Then she realized it was me. "Oh, never mind." She tried to act like I wasn't there and hurried on her way.

"Ember, wait," I called after her. And to my surprise, she actually stopped. She stood there for a moment with her back to me before slowly turning to face me.

"What is it, Chase?" she said flatly.

"I hate this," I said. "Can we just do whatever we need to and get back to the way things were before?" Ember crossed her arms and dropped her head, but remained silent. "I'm sorry for standing you up. I'm sorry I lost track of time and didn't meet you at the coffee shop. It wasn't on purpose and it doesn't mean I don't care about you."

"I know," Ember said quietly.

"And I didn't expect them to invite me in. I didn't expect that they'd want to talk to me for so long. If I'd known, then I wouldn't have —"

"It's okay," Ember interrupted. "You don't have to apologize. I shouldn't have gotten so upset."

"But I am sorry," I said. "I'm sorry if I did anything to make you feel like you aren't important."

"It wasn't your fault. I was just being ridiculous." Ember paused and took a deep breath. "The truth is, I was jealous. I *am* jealous. I have been ever since you first told me about Sophia. I don't want to be, I just...I am."

I didn't know how to respond. A thousand things raced through my mind, but none of them seemed like the right thing to say. I wanted some way to assure her, but I didn't want to embarrass her any more than she already seemed to be. The moment dragged on until I finally muttered the words, "I understand."

"You're the only real friend I have," Ember continued. "Not talking to you has been...tough."

"It has been for me too."

"I'm sorry I was jealous. And I'm sorry I was rude."

"It's okay," I said. "I know you just care about me."

"I do, but that's no excuse. You're a good friend, Chase. And I need to be better."

"Look, I'm willing to put all of this behind us and just start over. I need to talk to you. I need my friend."

The ice melted a bit and Ember smiled in a gentle, thankful way. "I want my friend to. And you're right. We do need to talk."

A wave of relief washed over me as I clapped my hands together and said, "So, we're good now? Everything is okay?"

"We're good," Ember said. Then she did something Ember had never done before. She reached out, grabbed me, and hugged me. A full-on hug, strong and desperate, like she was afraid to let go. She held me there like that for a moment before finally pulling away. "I'm really tired right now, so I'm going to bed. But we'll talk tomorrow, okay?"

"Yeah. Tomorrow. For sure."

I watched as Ember walked out of the glow of the campfires and was swallowed up by the darkness. It was tough for me to know what to make of the situation. I had known Ember for two years, but she was becoming more vulnerable than I had ever seen. It was clear that there was a lot I didn't know about Ember. A lot she'd never told me. But one thing I did know was that she hated looking weak. Ember was always tough. Always sure. To see her hurt and embarrassed was something new. Something unusual. And while I didn't know exactly what was whirling around inside of her head, I knew it had her all twisted up.

It suddenly dawned on me why I'd run into Ember in the first place. I was looking for the man in the green bow tie. I quickly glanced around, but I knew there was no use to continue my search. Wherever he was, it was surely far away from me. For a long time afterward, I questioned why I'd never reported what I'd seen. Normally, it would have been the first thing I'd have done. But there was something about the man that made me hold off. Even though I couldn't be certain, I didn't get the feeling he meant anyone harm. If he was up to no good, he would have had plenty of chances to act by that point. It seemed more like he was looking for something. Like he was there to observe. What he was looking for, I had no idea. But, twice he had seen me. Made eye contact with me. Twice he'd managed to make it onto the grounds and remain undetected. And, for what ever reason, I kept it quiet. I wanted to see how it would play out and if I'd get the chance to ask him myself what he was up.

That night, as I laid in my bed, my mind was racing. So much had happened so quickly that I wasn't able to process it all. I thought about Setu. And I couldn't shake the thought that what happened to him was my fault. I thought about Maya, the girl he loved and lost. His words were burned in my mind, *Not everyone comes here willingly.* Setu made it sound like he had been ripped from the life he loved and forced to be in the circus. It was the only time I'd ever heard anyone say something like that. But, if what he said was true, Setu didn't choose this life. Still, he served faithfully. But he made a mistake and wound up Forsaken. My heart ached for Setu. My mind then wandered to Cedric, the boy The Collector and I rescued from the hospital. Although I had no reason to doubt The Collector, I couldn't help but wonder if the story he'd told me about the boy was true. Was he really being abused? Was he in danger? The only way I'd know for sure was to ask Cedric as soon as I had the chance.

Ultimately my thoughts found their way to Sophia. Since the first time I met her, I'd had feelings for Sophia. She was strong and smart and kind. As we got to know each other, my feelings grew. But I'd always rejected the idea that she was more than a friend. I think maybe it was because I was scared to admit it. Most of my life was spent moving from place to place, family to family, school to school. Instinct told me if I never made close friends, I'd never feel the pain of losing them. Keeping a safe distance from people was like a shield that kept me from being hurt. If I didn't gain anything, I couldn't lose anything. Somewhere along the way, I must have made a mistake with Sophia because I was definitely feeling loss that night. I had allowed her to get too close. There was an ache in my chest to serve as a reminder to protect myself. And the thought that I'd never see her again was almost more than I could bear. Setu convinced me it was the right thing to do, but my heart told me I should have never gone to Sophia's house. It was like I had been given the perfect gift — one I'd been waiting on my whole life, and then I had it snatched away. The worst part about it was that there was no one to talk to. I certainly couldn't bring it up to Ember. Not now.

So, as I tossed and turned in my bed, trying to sleep, I made a decision that I'd never speak about Sophia again. I would do my best to erase her from my mind and move on. I'd pack her away like an old memory and bury the box for good. I wasn't sure if it was the right thing to do or not, or even if it was possible. But it was the only thought that brought me peace.

CHAPTER TEN

AT LEAST ONCE a week, after the shows were finished, The Collector would leave the circus and Analise would be in charge until he returned. There was a lot of talk about exactly where he would go and why, but the truth is none of us knew for sure. Some suspected he was out recruiting for the circus, which could be true, but I knew for a fact that Echo wasn't able to locate enough potential candidates to keep The Collector that busy. Others thought he might be out scouting different locations throughout time. Places we could set up our show. But for the two years I'd been with the circus, we kept a very strict schedule and always made our rounds to the same places and times. Always in order; always for a week at a time. Ember thought The Collector just wanted to get away from everything, that he probably had some cabin out in the wilderness far away from all the troubles of the circus. I wasn't sold on that idea. The Collector loved the circus. It was his family; he told us that over and over. He wasn't the type of leader who would ever feel the need to get away. And if Echo knew anything about why he left and where he went, he wasn't saying. He took his responsibility for discretion very seriously. I often thought no one was as loyal to the circus as Echo.

The next day was, as usual, filled with chores for everyone. Those of us who weren't performers were on a weekly rotation to make sure all daily responsibilities were completed and that the circus ran smoothly. That week, I was filling my least favorite role of all the jobs, cleaning up after the animals. Zuki was our animal keeper and a Prime who'd been with the circus for years. She was an odd old woman, hunched over and slow moving, with a keen mind and a strict, no nonsense approach to her work. While not many of us enjoyed working for Zuki, we did respect her and her unique ability. Zuki was able to communicate with the animals of the circus, and it was her job to ensure they were properly trained and cared for. Zuki had a thick accent, so I had to pay very close attention when she spoke. However, the work I did for her was typically simple and didn't require much explanation. I was there bright and early that day, still feeling the effects of a restless night. I was groggy and slow, but the sun was up and it was still cool outside so I was beginning to stir to life. As soon as I arrived Zuki was shuffling toward me, shovel in hand. She made a motion like she was teaching me how it worked. Her orders were sharp and direct. "You, you clean. You clean stall. Make empty."

"Got it," I mumbled as I took the shovel. It wasn't an ideal job, but at least I was starting with the zebras. I knew from experience that cleaning up after elephants or rhinos was no way to begin your morning.

I had been going at it long enough to gag at least twice, when Ember showed up. "Quite the niche you've carved out here, buddy," she said as she stepped up behind me. "I never knew you had such a love for animals. You and Echo must have loads to talk about."

"Real funny," I said as I tossed a shovel full of zebra dung toward her. She nearly gagged but managed to scoot aside. "Not all of us can be headliners you know? Someone has to scoop the poop."

"Well, I, for one, believe it is a noble calling," she said with a grin. "It suits you well."

It was nice to see Ember in a good mood. I seemed like it had been a long time since we'd had a normal conversation. One that didn't result in an argument or hurt feelings. "So did you need something or did you just want to make fun of me?" I said playfully.

"No, I don't really need anything. And making fun of you is just a bonus."

Zuki finally looked up from her work to notice Ember was there. Knowing Zuki, I expected her to be upset that Ember was distracting me. I assumed she'd begin one of her infamous rants, striking out in a language neither of us would understand. Or, at the very least, tell Ember to get lost. Instead, Zuki smiled a huge toothy grin and held up wiggling fingers as she called out, "Fire girl. Fire girl."

"Hi, Zuki," Ember said, waving. "How's the baby giraffe?"

If Zuki understood Ember's question, she didn't answer. She just kept smiling and repeating the same words as before. "Fire girl. Fire girl." She went on like that for a moment before finally deciding to continue her chores while joyfully muttering to herself.

"It must be nice having fans everywhere you go," I said as I continued to shovel.

Ember ignored my comment. "The Collector left again last night."

"Oh, yeah?" I said. "That's nothing new."

"I know, but I wonder what he does when leaves."

"Whatever it is, I'm sure it's a lot more fun than this," I said, motioning to the wheelbarrow.

"Do you think he goes out to check on all the Forsaken?" Ember said.

"Check on them? They're Forsaken. That's the whole point, isn't it? Why would he check on them when he's the one who got rid of them?"

"I don't know, but he has to still care about them, right?"

I stopped my work and leaned against my shovel. "Maybe." I paused. "Ember, I feel terrible about Setu. I feel like he was Forsaken because of us. Or really, because of me."

"I know," she said dropping her head. "But it wasn't all your fault. I'm just as much to blame as you. I know everyone says he made his own choice, but I still feel awful."

"I asked Echo if he could find any records that would tell us where the Forsaken were sent."

"Yeah, so did I," she said. "I'm guessing he didn't tell you either."

I shook my head. "You know how Echo is. I don't think he'd ever do anything like that, but I thought it was worth a try."

"I could sneak in and try to find the files myself," Ember said.

"Yeah, right. Do you even know how to use a computer?"

"No, but how hard can it be? If Echo can figure it out, I'm sure I can."

"You underestimate Echo," I said. "Besides, he never had to *figure* it out. All he had to do was touch the thing to understand it. He may be a little weird, but the kid has a gift."

"Okay, okay," Ember said. "But we have to figure something out. We can't just leave Setu out there trapped in some strange place. We have to find a way to help him. To get him back. Or maybe help him get him back to Maya."

"It's a waste of time," I said. "The Collector's the only one who'd be able to find him or help him. It was his decision to send Setu away. He's not just going to bring him back because we ask. You know it doesn't work like that."

"Maybe we should talk to The Collector. See if we can change his mind."

"I don't know if that's a good idea. We barely managed to stay out of trouble ourselves. Maybe we should just drop it."

Ember narrowed her eyes at me. "So you're saying you're okay with leaving Setu where he is? Forsaken? He's our friend, Chase. He's like family."

I took a deep breath and released it slowly. Ember was right. I had spent most of my life believing in the idea of every man for himself. It didn't always come naturally for me to think of others as family. "I'm sorry. You're right. If you think talking to The Collector will help, then let's give it a shot."

"Good," Ember said with a nod. "We'll have to figure it out later though. I can't handle the smell of this place anymore."

Zuki called out her goodbyes as Ember walked away waving. I pulled my shirt up over my nose and kept shoveling.

～⑤～

I was six years old, hiding in my bedroom closet, listening to the Millers scream at each other and throw things around the house. For a little over three months I was with them and every weekend had been the same. During the week we were a typical family. We got up, ate breakfast, went to school, came home, ate dinner, did homework, and went to bed. But, when the weekend came around, Mr. Miller would stay out late, usually not coming home until everyone in the house was asleep. Most nights it was his shuffling around in the kitchen and digging through the refrigerator that would wake me up. Something would drop or break and he'd curse. My eyes would pop open and I'd pull the covers up over my head. I knew what would happen next. Mrs. Miller would get up, enter the kitchen, and start yelling about how terrible a person and father he was for coming home drunk again. Sometimes the arguing would end quickly, but other times it would drag on for what felt like hours. That particular night, the fighting went on long enough that hiding under the covers wasn't enough to provide the comfort I needed. I took my blanket and ran to my closet, shut myself inside, and tried to cover my ears. As usual, it didn't help. Even though we were separated by several walls and my hands were cupped tightly over my ears, I could still hear them fighting.

"I'm sick of the way you treat us," I heard Mrs. Miller scream in between the crashing of what sounded like dishes being thrown. "I can't live like this anymore. I'm packing up, taking Sarah and Chase and we are leaving." Sarah was the Miller's biological daughter. She was just a baby at the time. Being so young, Sarah didn't understand what was happening and would usually sleep through the ruckus. I often thought she was the lucky one.

"You're not going anywhere," Mr. Miller yelled back. Although I was hidden away in my closet, I could picture his swollen red face, the vein popping out in his neck, and his glassy eyes filled with hate. I'd seen him like that several times before and the image was burned into my mind. I was terrified of the man, and I usually did everything I could to stay away from him.

"Get your hands off me," she called out. There was a scuffle, followed by some inaudible shrieks and a heavy thud.

Everything went quiet.

After a few moments of silence, I became concerned enough that I crawled out of my hiding place and crept toward the kitchen. When I peaked around the corner from the hallway, I saw Mr. Miller standing over his wife who was lying motionless on the floor. He didn't check on her. He didn't ask if she was okay or call for help. He just stood there looking down at her as if his shoes were stuck to the floor. There was a dull, blank look on his face and his fists were clinched at his side.

"Mr. Miller," I said quietly. They told me it was alright if I wanted to call him dad, but it never felt right. He didn't hear me. He just stood there still. Staring down at his wife. I spoke louder. "Mr. Miller, is she alright?"

He turned his cold eyes to mine and glared at me like he

wasn't really there at all. He was an empty shell of a person. A dried-out husk filled with hatred and rage. "Get out of here, Chase," he said in a low, calm voice. Everything in me wanted to run, but I was frozen in place. My feet wouldn't budge. Then, Mr. Miller turned on me and screamed as loud as he could, "I said, *get out.*"

The volume of his words and the anger in his tone shook something free inside of me. My legs began to work again, and I raced back to my room, ducked under the covers, and wrapped them tightly around me. I stayed that way for quite a while, hoping and praying that the night would pass quickly. Wondering if Mrs. Miller was safe. At some point during the early morning hours, as I laid there curled up into a ball, I managed to fall asleep despite the fear that swallowed me. When I woke up the next morning, my social worker was at the house with two police officers. We talked briefly about things I later couldn't recall, and she loaded me into an old, black car and had me wait. No one ever told me what happened to Mrs. Miller, or whether or not she was okay. We simply drove off as I stared out of the backseat window. The house grew smaller and smaller until eventually it was completely out of view. I never saw or spoke to the Millers again.

No one had officially told me that I was allowed to visit Cedric in the infirmary. Then again, no one told me I couldn't. The boy had been on my mind ever since The Collector and I had rescued him from the hospital. So, after Zuki let me go for the day, I went to check in on him. When I arrived, there were no doctors or nurses to be found. Apparently everyone had stepped out for a moment, and since I could practically see Cedric from where I stood, I decided to duck in quickly. I figured I could be in and out before anyone knew I was there.

Cedric looked to be sleeping as I entered. It was dark inside the infirmary with only a small, dim lamp burning beside his bed. Most of Cedric's bruises and wounds had healed, and he looked like any other six-year-old boy should. I quietly made my way to his bedside and laid a hand on his shoulder. "Cedric," I whispered. "Cedric, are you awake?"

The young boy's eyes immediately sprang open and he glared at me with a wide-eyed, hesitant expression. "Who are you?" he said, squinting to adjust to the dim light.

"My name's Chase," I replied softly. "I was the one who came and got you. From the hospital."

"That was you?"

"Yes, me and The Collector. We were both there."

"I didn't want to leave," Cedric said. His voice began to shake. "I want to go back home."

"I know you don't understand all of this." I pulled up a chair and sat down beside him. "I know it's all very confusing, but you can trust us. You can trust me. We're trying to help you."

Cedric was beginning to panic. "I don't need your help. I want my mom and dad. I want to go home."

"I know, Cedric," I said, doing my best to calm him. "I understand. But your dad…he wasn't a very nice person. He was mean to you."

"No, he wasn't," Cedric said, his forehead wrinkled. "My dad isn't mean to anybody."

"But I saw your bruises. I know what he did to you. I know about the baseball bat."

Cedric looked genuinely confused. He sat up a little in his bed and grimaced from the pain of the movement. "Baseball bat?"

I glanced around the room to make sure we were still alone. "It was your dad who did this to you. He came home drunk again and beat you with a baseball bat because you spilled juice."

"That's not true," Cedric said. "My dad doesn't drink. He's the pastor at our church. He would never hit me."

"If it wasn't your dad, then what happened to you? How did you get all of those bruises?"

"I was on my bike riding on the sidewalk. A car came around the corner and they were shooting out of the window at someone. I tried to get out of the way, but the car ran up on the sidewalk and hit me. When I woke up, I was in the hospital. They asked me who I was and who my parents were. I don't remember much more, but then I woke up here."

My body tingled and my mouth went numb. How could Cedric's story be true? And if it was, then The Collector had lied to me. But why would he? There was no reason to lie. I tried to speak, but the words wouldn't come to me. "Cedric, I…"

"Can you help me?" Cedric said, desperation in his eyes. "Can you help me get back to my parents? They have to be worried about me."

"Cedric, I don't know what to say. I'm not sure what —"

"Please," Cedric said. His eyes were filling with tears. "Please take me home."

"You can't be in here," a voice called from the doorway. It was a large man wearing scrubs and carrying a clipboard. "What's your name?"

I didn't give the man a chance to ask anything else. I jumped up and ran right past him and out of the infirmary. The man yelled for me to stop and chased me for a bit, but I managed to lose him. I ran until I nearly collapsed behind one of the tents, gasping for air and trying to make sense of everything Cedric had told me. But I had looked into his eyes and I believed everything he said. I couldn't understand why The Collector lied to me, but I knew I had to find out.

CHAPTER ELEVEN

THAT NIGHT AFTER the show, Ember, Echo and I sat around the campfire as usual. I told them about going to see Cedric and how the story he gave me didn't line up with The Collector's. Ember wasn't convinced there was a problem. She said I had to remember that Cedric didn't know everything The Collector knew. Cedric only knew what was happening in his present and he could only see the past through his own filter. She was sure that since he was only six years old, he couldn't understand everything that happened. I wasn't sure I agreed. We talked about it until there was nothing left to say. But, even though the conversation had lulled and Ember and I were quietly lost in our thoughts, Echo was in full information sharing mode. Unfortunately, that information was based on his recent study of the emperor penguin.

"Fun fact about their diving habits," Echo began.

"No," Ember said. "It isn't a fun fact. And neither were the last twelve. We don't care about penguins."

Echo went on as if he didn't realize Ember had spoken at all. "Most people don't realize they are incredible divers. In fact, the deepest dive on record is over ninety feet."

"So, let me get this straight," Ember said. "You're telling

me some guy actually went down to the Antarctic to measure how deep a penguin can dive?"

Echo nodded. "I'm sure he was involved in some other experimental studies though, probably part of a team."

"Sounds like a cool job," I said.

"It sounds amazing," Echo replied.

"Absolutely," Ember said, her voice thick with sarcasm. "Maybe we should check into that for you, Echo. Sounds like a great birthday present. You being in Antarctica for a year or two. Let's make that happen."

Echo raised a finger before speaking. "As amazing as that gift would be, I'm afraid The Collector would never allow me to be gone from —"

"Yeah, we get it, Echo," Ember cut in. "Anyway, Chase, I still think Cedric was confused. He was beat up pretty badly."

Apparently, there was more to the story she wanted to discuss. "He didn't seem confused. He was very clear about how much he loved his parents and wanted to go home."

Echo didn't offer anything. He just sat there looking uncomfortable and fidgeting with the zipper on his jacket. "Echo," Ember said, noticing his discomfort. "Do you know anything about this? About Cedric?"

Echo shifted around before eventually releasing an overly exaggerated yawn. "I'm getting really tired, guys," he said as he stood. "I should probably turn in."

"You're tired?" Ember said. "You've talked non-stop about penguins for the last thirty minutes, and just when you have something we actually want to hear, you're tired?"

"Let him go," I said. Echo raced away like his clothes were on fire.

"Let him go?" Ember said, echoing me. "He knows something."

"I know he does, but he can't tell us. It's not fair for us to pressure him."

Ember groaned and dropped back on the stump she'd been leaning against. "Why can't he just be normal?"

I laughed despite myself. "Ember, look around. None of us are normal. You emit fire from your body and are part of a time traveling group of circus performers. I think we all signed up for abnormal."

"Yeah, but it's frustrating. Everything we want to know is right there on the computer. And Echo could easily find out."

"It's not fair though," I said. "Look what happened to the last person who tried to help us."

"I know. You're right. I'm just tired of feeling helpless." Ember paused. "The Collector should be back sometime tonight. Maybe we should go see him first thing tomorrow. Get some answers. Or at least try."

At that moment, a rowdy cheer rose up from one of the nearby campfires. We turned our heads to get a better look and spotted a large crowd of circus folk gathered around the fire where the knife thrower, Julius, and his son, Tobin, hung out at night. "Let's go see what's happening," I said. So Ember and I raced toward the crowd, pushing our way through to get a better look.

"Ladies and gentlemen," Julius called out. He was waving his hands with great fanfare. "Tonight we had an amazing show. All of us. But I'm afraid I wasn't able to demonstrate the full extent of my talents, and I simply hate to deprive you good men and women of a truly magnificent display."

He held up a half empty bottle and took a huge gulp. "So, tonight, after having quite a few sips of this glorious elixir, I shall attempt a feat worthy of my skills and your attention." The group cheered and Julius made a great show of bowing in all directions. He was a wiry man with a few patches of facial hair and a ponytail that kept his jet black hair out of his eyes. Julius always had a dark tan, and I wasn't sure if it was reflective of his ethnicity or because he went around shirtless most of the year. His skin was thick and leathery and his torso and arms were covered in tattoos of all different colors and designs. Tobin, his son, was nearly as precocious as his father, but only half the size. They looked very much alike except for the fact that Tobin wasn't quite old enough for facial hair and he typically wore a shirt. "I believe we'll begin with a simple card trick," Julius continued as he pulled a deck of cards from his pocket. "Can I get a volunteer from the audience?"

"Oh, pick me," Ember said, her hand shooting up.

"The fire girl," Julius announced. "Step right up, miss."

I grabbed Ember's arm and whispered in her ear. "Ember, are you sure about this? I think he's been drinking."

"Don't worry," she said with a grin. "I'll be fine. People shoot cannons at me, remember?" Ember pulled away and moved next to Julius, curtsying to the delight of the crowd.

"I hold in my hand a simple deck of cards," Julius said. He was slurring his words a bit, and he nearly dropped the cards as he held them up for everyone to see. "Now, Ember, if you will, inspect these cards and confirm that there is no trickery involved here."

Ember shuffled through the deck, carefully inspecting it

before announcing to the crowd, "They're just normal cards. No...trickery."

"Thank you, lovely Ember," Julius continued. "Now if you will choose a single card from the deck, hold it high above your head, and show everyone which card you hold." Ember did just as he asked, holding up the two of diamonds.

"Now, please let me see your card," Julius said. The crowed laughed and Ember held the card to her chest.

"I can't show you my card," she said. "It'll ruin the trick."

"Ah, my dear," Julius said tilting his head, the movement of which almost made him lose his balance. "I assure you this trick will astound and amaze. Trust me."

"So, you want to see the card?"

"Please, madame." Ember held up the card for Julius to take a look. "Oh, the two of diamonds. Nice choice. I am told ladies love diamonds. Perhaps someday a lucky gentleman will give you one of your own."

Ember shrugged, and a puff of flame came off her shoulders. "I can make my own."

Julius continued as he took a careful step back. "Here's what I want you to do, Ember. On the count of three, I want you to take the deck of cards and throw them high into the air above your head. Do you think you can do that?"

"I can do that," Ember said, grinning.

"Alright, everyone count with me." The crowd joined in as Julius called out, "One...two...Oh wait a moment, I nearly forgot." The crowd collectively chuckled at the showmanship. "Tobin, my boy, come and take your spot here, please." Tobin came forward, carrying a small block of wood. He laid down on the ground at Julius's feet and placed the block on his chest. He shifted around like he was trying to make sure he was in exactly the right spot. "Alright, let's try this again," Julius said to Ember before throwing his head back and taking a huge gulp from the bottle he was still holding. "Remember, on three." And again the crowd joined in with him, "One…two…three."

Ember threw the deck of cards high above her head. They fanned out and flew in all directions like confetti at a parade. What happened next, happened so quickly, I barely saw it. Julius reached to his side, pulled a long, thin knife from its sheath, and threw it straight up over his head. Ember moved aside, but Julius held his ground, his eyes fixed on the knife. It spun around overhead, whizzing through the night air and, on it's descent, pierced one of the cards before sticking, with a penetrating thud, into the block of wood resting on Tobin's chest.

There was a collective gasp and everyone stood in awe for a moment as Julius leaned over to pull the knife from the block. The card was still stuck on the blade. He staggered and fell to one knee, but jumped up quickly, brandishing the knife with clownish showboating. "Never fear," he yelped. "I do some of my best work while slightly glazed." There were a few chuckles, but seeing him wave the knife around made most of us a little anxious. "Ember, will you please remove the card from the blade and show everyone what you see? Carefully, now. It's very sharp."

Ember hesitantly reached out and pulled the card from the knife Julius held in his shaky hand. She looked at the card, then at Julius, and a timid smile stretched across her face. Then Ember shot her hand up, holding the card for all of us to see. The two of diamonds. Cheers erupted from the circus members as Julius took a clumsy bow. "Thank you. Thank you, my good people," Julius called out. "Now for my next trick, I will need another volunteer. Someone with nerves of steel and the heart of a lion."

Ember raced over to me and pushed me forward. "Chase volunteers," she said. The crowed applauded me, which made it impossible for everyone to hear my rejection. Unfortunately, I had been pulled forward by Julius and handed a blindfold before I even had the chance to say no.

"Welcome to the the stage, Chase," Julius said. He took another swig from his bottle and tossed it aside. "Let's hear it for Chase everyone. He's one of our most promising Evos." I glared at Ember as the crowd applauded, but it didn't seem to bother her much. She hooted and yelled alongside everyone else. "Chase, in your hand you hold a blindfold." I began to lift the blindfold up to cover my eyes, but Julius stopped me. "No, Chase, the blindfold is not for you, it's for me," Julius said before announcing, "Tobin, bring me my blades." Tobin appeared with a large leather case that he unfolded to reveal six daggers, each about a foot long.

My stomach dropped. "Julius, is this is a good idea?"

Julius ignored my comment. "Now, Chase, please take the blindfold and tie it around my eyes." Julius bent down in front of me and nearly toppled over. The smell of alcohol on his breath was strong. I hesitated, but my friends and circus members urged me on with their shouts of support. I had seen Julius do many amazing things in his show, and I couldn't deny his talent. But I wondered if his drinking had dulled his abilities. Glancing out at the others, they didn't seemed too concerned, so I placed the blindfold around Julius' eyes and tied it behind his head.

As soon as I'd finished, Julius stood up and Tobin slid a thick wooden board behind me. A large "X" was painted over the board and it was covered in gashes. Tobin gently nudged me backwards until I was standing with my back pressed against the board. He lifted both of my arms out to the side and motioned for me to spread my legs apart as well. It was at that moment, I made the decision I couldn't go through with it. I couldn't let a drunk man wearing a blindfold throw knives at me. However, before I could move, thin metal shackles slid out of the board securing my hands and feet in place. I struggled against the restraints, but it was no use. I was trapped. I searched the crowd looking for Ember, thinking surely she'd help me. But when I finally caught her gaze, she was clapping and smiling along with everyone else. She mouthed the words, "Don't worry." I knew the impromptu show was happening whether I wanted it to or not.

Julius was, as he called it, thoroughly glazed by the time he decided he'd throw knives at me. I could have shouted, fought, kicked, or generally thrown a fit, but I didn't want to look like a scared child in front of everyone. Especially when I considered the fact they were all so impressive and I was still waiting to discover my abilities. So, I decided to shut my eyes tight and trust in Julius' talent. "Tobin, please do the honor of spinning me around three times and pointing me in the general direction of my...target." From that point on, I didn't see what happened. It was only later when Ember filled me in on all the details that I was truly able to cringe at the riskiness of it all.

Tobin spun the staggering Julius around three times before aiming him at me. As Julius wobbled back on his heels before falling again, he threw one of the knives. It sank deep into the wooden board just over my right hand. The loud thud startled me, and I peeked just long enough to get a good look at the blade that barely missed my thumb. Everyone was loud. Nonstop laughter and cheers. If it wasn't for the fact that they were all accustomed to such dangerous acts, it would have seemed cruel. But because they were all powerful individuals, watching Julius throw knives at me was more like entertainment for them. They didn't interpret danger the way most people did. The way I did. They weren't as vulnerable as I was.

Apparently, Tobin helped Julius to his feet because it was only a few seconds before Julius was making an announcement to the crowd. "Pardon my slip up folks, but inebriation does have its pitfalls." He paused for laughter as if he was rehearsing a show. "For my next feat, I will throw two knives at once. However, this time, I shall face the opposite direction. Assuming Tobin follows my instructions that is. Tobin, if you please."

Tobin again spun Julius around a few times, bringing him to a halt with his back to me. Without hesitation, Julius threw two knives, one from each hand, backwards over his shoulders. They hit nearly simultaneously, the first jabbed into the board a couple of inches from my right ear, and the second nicked my left ear before sticking in place. I immediately felt a sting and a thin stream of blood dripping from my earlobe. I began to pull against my restraints, but it was no use. I would be there until someone released me. Everyone moaned a collective, "Ohhh," and Julius immediately began his explanation.

"No need to be overly concerned," he began. "I can tell by sound of the blade that I must have pricked some flesh. But then again, where would the theatrics lie without the threat of peril? I assure you the boy will be fine."

It was at that moment, the crowd began to chant, "Three for one. Three for one. Three for one." I had no idea what it meant, but it sounded dangerous.

"The people have spoken," Julius cried out.

Then another voice cut through the noise, silencing the crowd. "That's enough," Ember said. I opened my eyes for the second time. "You've been drinking and you've already hurt him. This is over."

"But the Three for One is my showpiece," Julius said, opening his arms wide. "The jewel of my act. Three blades, thrown at the same time, with all three tips striking the exact same mark. Surely you're interested in witnessing such a feat."

"I'm not," Ember said. "Now let him go."

"But the people have demanded it. We cannot disappoint."

"I don't care what the people want. *Let him go.* Last warning."

It was a warning Julius didn't heed. His only response was a crooked smile before moving so quickly Ember had no time to react. Julius turned on a dime and threw all three knives at me. I pressed my eyes shut tightly and gritted my teeth. But the impact never came. There was no pain, so I knew the blades hadn't hit me. But there was no thud, so I also knew they hadn't lodged into the board. And as I stood there wincing in that seemingly endless moment, I also noticed the silence. Silence like I'd never heard before. Total and complete. I imagined it must be how floating in space would sound. Totally enveloping. I wondered if maybe Julius had accidentally killed me. That I was gone and that was how it felt to be dead. To no longer exist.

When I finally got the nerve to force my eyes open, I saw the world like I'd never seen it before. I struggled to make sense of it. It was like I was standing in the middle of a television show that had been paused. The air was heavy and thick. It pressed against me, making it difficult to move, difficult to breathe. Even the movement of my eyes seemed to push against the air like it was thick — solidified. And there, right in front of my face, were all three knives. They were suspended there, hanging less than an inch from my face. The blades had sliced the night sky, tearing through the air around them, leaving a trail like water off the wake of a boat.

Then the still, silence of that moment was suddenly interrupted by a voice that boomed like thunder. "Brazen fool," The Collector said as he reached out and plucked the knifes right out of the space in front of me. He tossed them aside and they fell heavily against the earth with a sound that made it seem they were made of iron. "Let me guess, our dear friend Julius has been drinking again. Had I not shown up when I did, he might have killed you."

CHAPTER TWELVE

"You really need to do what he says without talking back," Mrs. Jennings said in her most helpful tone. I suppose she was a kind enough lady, but truthfully I thought she was a wimp. Her husband, Clyde, had to be the most horrible person I'd ever met. Clyde. Even his name made me cringe. The Jennings were hands down my least favorite family to ever be placed with. Not once did I hear a kind word come out of Clyde's mouth unless I count the time Mrs. Jennings asked if he liked the spaghetti. He looked up, grunted and kept shoveling it in.

"If he wasn't so mean, I wouldn't talk back," I said as I finished off my last spoonful of cereal.

"You have to understand," she said, leaning in closer. We were sitting at the kitchen table, having breakfast before I had to leave for school. "Clyde works very hard. And when he comes home after a long day's work, he wants his house to be clean and peaceful."

"Well, he's the only one around here who's not peaceful."

"All he asks is for you to show him respect and —"

"All I ask is not to get smacked in the face."

Mrs. Jennings fiddled with her necklace. "Look, I know Clyde isn't a perfect man, but he's a good man. And he —"

"Is he though?"

"Yes, Chase, he is. He has his problems, but so does everyone else. No one is perfect. Including you. Including me."

"I can't believe you're actually taking up for him," I said as I pushed my empty bowl away. I pointed to the faint bruise along my left jawline that was still visible even after a week. "Look at my face. You remember this, right?" Mrs. Jennings looked away. "He slapped me in the face because I asked for ten dollars to go on a field trip."

"Like I said, he's not perfect," Mrs. Jennings said, turning a slight shade of pink. "He makes mistakes like everyone else."

"But it's not like everyone else. His mistakes show up on my face."

Mrs. Jennings stood up quickly and raised her voice. "That's enough. Clyde is a good man. We take you in. We feed you; take care of you. Provide you with a good education. And all you want to do is talk poorly of my husband."

I'd gone too far, and I knew I'd better start backing off quickly. "You're right. I'm sorry. I shouldn't have said those things."

"You should be sorry. Where would you be now if it wasn't for us?"

"I — I don't know."

"It's shameful the way you speak to us. And I will not allow such talk to take place in —"

"What's going on in here?" Clyde said as he stomped

into the kitchen. His gravelly voice cut through the kitchen like a dull blade.

"Nothing, Clyde," Mrs. Jennings said rather unconvincingly. She moved over to the sink and began washing dishes she'd already washed.

Clyde stepped up to the table and I dropped my eyes. "You have something to say to me, boy?"

"No, sir," I replied. It was my standard reply anytime Clyde asked me a question. My whole body was tense. Every muscle strained. I'd been in that situation before. Afraid to speak. Afraid to move. I knew the tone he'd get, the look in his eye. The way his hand would twitch before he decided to hit me.

"Stand up," he said. I didn't move. Clyde raised his voice. "You want to be a tough guy and talk about me when I'm not around. So stand up and say what you have to say."

Still, I didn't move. "I don't have anything to say, sir."

"I said, stand up." Clyde kicked the leg of my chair with such force that it collapsed beneath me and I tumbled onto the floor. Mrs. Jennings began screaming for Clyde to stop. To calm down.

He didn't.

Mrs. Jennings moved between us. She placed her hands on Clyde's chest, pleading with him to sit down and let her make him breakfast. He had no intention of stopping. Clyde wanted to teach me a lesson, to show me he was the man of the house. With a swipe of his arm, he threw Mrs. Jennings aside as easily as someone might toss a paper ball at a trashcan. She ended up across the kitchen from me, sprawled out on the tile floor, crying and begging Clyde to stop. The last thing I saw that day was the terrified look on her tear-stained face. Only for a moment though. Clyde's fist came down on the side of my head. I woke up the next day in the hospital bruised and swollen. It wasn't all bad though. The best thing to come out of it was that I never set foot in the Jennings' home again.

✑

"How did this happen, Chase?" The Collector asked as we made our way to the infirmary. I was holding my ear and my hand was covered in blood.

"I don't know. One minute we were watching Julius and Tobin do some tricks, and the next I was strapped to a board while he threw knives at me. It wasn't something we planned. It all just sort of…happened."

The Collector pushed aside the curtain to the infirmary and marched in with me close behind. The doctors and nurses leaped to attention, asking if they could help. With a wave of his hand, The Collector dismissed them and led me to an empty bed just inside the entrance. I glanced over to where I had visited Cedric earlier. The bed was empty, neatly made, and Cedric was nowhere to be found.

"Take a seat, Chase," The Collector said as he rolled up his sleeves.

"Sir, where is Cedric? Is he still here? Is he better?"

A young woman in scrubs stepped up behind The Collector as he gathered and organized a supply of stainless steel instruments. "Would you like me to do that for you, sir?" the young woman said. "I can take over if you'd like."

"That won't be necessary," The Collector replied. "I can manage." The woman turned and looked at me with troubled eyes before reluctantly leaving. The Collector carried on, readying his supplies before taking out a syringe which he held up to his eyes and thumped. "This might sting a bit," he said as he moved closer. He gave me a shot just below my ear; I only winced a little. "Alright," he said, "That wasn't so bad was it?"

"No, it was fine," I said.

"It looks like you're going to need a couple of stitches," he said as he went on readying the supplies. "Do you mind if I do the honors? I assure you I have been well-trained."

"That's fine with me," I said. Truthfully I wasn't so sure, but it was hard for any of us to say no to The Collector. "Do you know where Cedric is? Is he okay?"

"Cedric is perfectly fine," The Collector said. "We were able to move him on earlier today." He said the words so casually. Like it was no more important than the toast he had for breakfast.

"Move him on?"

"Yes, I didn't want to mention it because I didn't want to upset you or cause you to feel responsible in any way. But it seems as if we made a mistake. Based on Echo's information, we believed Cedric possessed certain weather-related abilities. Unfortunately, we were incorrect."

"So since he doesn't have any abilities, he was kicked out?"

The Collector cocked his head to the side and looked at me like I'd just challenged him with a riddle. "No, Chase. He wasn't kicked out. We bring people into the circus to protect them, to give them a safe place to practice their abilities, to teach them how to use them. When it became clear to me that Cedric didn't possess any abilities, and that his being here would serve no purpose, I chose to relocate him."

"But part of the reason I decided we should take him was to keep him safe," I said. "His family is dangerous. You said they can't take care of him. He'll die if we leave him there."

"Please, Chase, have a little faith," The Collector said. "I would never take Cedric somewhere unsafe. Not after the way we disrupted his life. I made sure Cedric was placed with a wonderful family who'll love him as their own. He will have a far better life because of what we did for him. What you did. You should feel good about your decision."

I nodded and laid back on the table as The Collector began to stitch me up. By that time, my ear was completely numb so there was no pain. He spoke to me as he worked, moving deliberately and carefully. "I do appreciate your concern for Cedric. It's refreshing to see someone who cares for others, considering how selfish this world can be. But how have you been doing, Chase? Have your sessions with Olivia been going well?"

"I think so. But she hasn't found my ability yet. She thinks we will soon. I only hope she's right."

"Well, Olivia is seldom wrong. She's been with the circus for years now. If an ability's there, she'll find it."

I hesitated, searching for the right words. "But, if she doesn't…If she isn't able to find an ability…"

The Collector stopped his work for a moment. He backed away and looked into my eyes. "What is it, Chase? What's bothering you?"

"If Olivia doesn't find my ability soon, will I have to be Forsaken? Will I be sent away like Setu?"

The Collector smiled with kind eyes and gently placed the instruments on the tray. "Chase, I want you to understand something. Setu was made a Forsaken because he betrayed my trust. There are certain nonnegotiable aspects of working security. I make sure our team is fully aware of the serious nature of their positions. I am very clear about the consequences for failing to live up to their commitment. And more importantly, I always follow through with enforcing the rules that keep this circus safe. Setu made it impossible for me to keep him here. He knows a great deal about the circus — about how we operate, our strengths and weaknesses. When he made it clear my trust was misplaced, I had to take the necessary steps to protect us." He placed a hand on my arm. "I know Setu was your friend. He was mine as well. And believe me, if there had been a way to keep him without breaking the very rules meant to protect us, I would have. There simply wasn't another option."

"Where did you send him?" I knew he wouldn't answer.

"I sent him somewhere that will ensure his safety as well as ours." The Collector took up the instruments once again, moved closer to me, and went to work stitching my ear.

"And what about me? What are the rules for people like me? Those who don't manifest soon enough?"

"I'm not sure what rumors you may have heard about Evos," The Collector said as he worked. "About them being Forsaken because they take too long to discover their abilities. But I wouldn't put too much weight on such stories."

"So you won't send me away? Even if I don't have an ability?"

Again, The Collector pulled away and looked at me with great concern. "Chase, as I have told you since the first night you arrived, you are family now. This circus, these people, we belong to you and you belong to us. I believe in you. Olivia believes in you. It *will* happen. I want you to rest easily. I have no intention of seeing this circus continue without your being a part of it."

Something about his words stirred up a sense of peace inside me. Though I grew up pushing the thought away, I'd always wanted to feel cared about, to feel like I belonged. The Collector had given me that. He gave me a purpose. He gave me a family. "Thank you, sir," I said. "I'm going to work hard to find my ability so I can do my part for the circus. So I can contribute."

The Collector smiled and tousled my hair. "I have no doubt you will, Chase." He stood and tossed his latex gloves in the trash. "I think we're done here. Keep that clean and covered up for a day or two and it should be fine. Come back in a week and one of the nurses will take the stitches out for you."

"I will. Thank you."

The Collector walked toward the door, paused, and then came back over to me. "Can I talk to you about something? Since we're just chatting?"

"Sure," I said, hoping I wasn't in some sort of trouble.

"Tell me about the girl."

"The girl?"

"The girl you visited on your day away from the circus. What was her name?"

"Oh, you mean Sophia." I wondered for a moment how he knew I'd visited someone, but then realized The Collector probably knew just about everything that went on.

He nodded. "Yes, that's it. Sophia. Tell me…how do you know her?"

"She's just a friend from school. You know, before the circus."

"I understand. We all had lives before the circus." He paused. "I'm curious, was the girl part of the reason Setu helped you and Ember sneak away?"

I dropped my eyes and nodded. "She was."

The Collector sat on the foot of the bed. "It's alright, Chase. I'm not blaming you for anything that happened. I was simply inquiring. Did Setu ever talk to you about the girl? Sophia?"

"No, sir," I said. "All he told me was to make sure I didn't have any regrets. That I should talk to her if I got the chance."

The Collector furrowed his brow and seemed to stare off toward something that wasn't there. Something I couldn't see. But in an instant, the concern seemed to dissolve into a confident, beaming smile. "It's a terrible thing to live with regrets."

"Setu thought so," I said. "But you don't have to worry about things like that, do you?"

"What do you mean?" The Collector said.

"Well, if you regret something, can't you just go back in time and undo it? Make it right? Start over?"

The Collector smiled and dropped his head. "Were it

only that simple." With one last pat on the leg, The Collector left me there in the infirmary. As I was trying to decide whether or not I should wait for an actual nurse, or if I should just leave, Ember quickly ducked inside.

"I'm sorry, Chase," she said racing over to me. "I'm sorry I didn't stop Julius sooner. I thought he was just goofing around. If I'd known he was going to —"

"It's okay, Ember," I interrupted. "You didn't know."

"Well, still…I'm sorry. I won't happen again."

"Did you hear anything The Collector and I were talking about?"

"Ahh…I sort of heard all of it," Ember said turning up the corner of her mouth. "I was standing right outside the door. I hope that's okay."

"It's fine." We sat there in silence for a moment. "I asked him about Setu. I tried to find out where —"

"I heard," Ember said. "I don't know what else we can do. If we push anymore we could end up in serious trouble."

"And then there's Cedric. I guess we'll never know what happened to him either."

"Or if he was telling the truth."

There was a part of me that was relieved. I had worked my whole life to find a home, friends, to feel safe. I was afraid that if we kept questioning everything the way we had been, I'd lose it. I couldn't lose it. "Maybe it's for the best," I said.

Ember twisted up her face like she was wrestling with whether or not that was true. "Maybe. I just wish there was someone who knew more. Or at least someone who could tell us where Setu is and if he's safe."

A voice came from the doorway. "I know where he is."

We both turned to look at the young, awkward boy standing there looking scared to death. "And I know where Cedric is too." It was the last person we expected to offer us anything at all. Echo.

CHAPTER THIRTEEN

MAKING FRIENDS WAS difficult moving around as much as I did. Middle school was especially tough. Many of my days were spent sitting alone in the cafeteria or praying that my teacher wouldn't assign a project that forced me into some group that would rather not have me. The eye rolls and snickering was almost more than I could bear, and when I had the choice, I kept to myself. The only friend I had was Victor, and it wasn't like he was going to help me fit in. Victor was nearly as much of an outcast as I was, except for the fact that it didn't seem to bother him. I don't think he even noticed. Victor was friendly, loud, and completely oblivious to most things going on around him. He was the first person I met when my family forced me to go to that party when I was twelve. But the party was also where I met Sophia, so I guess it wasn't all bad. I spoke to Sophia every now and then when I'd pass her in the hallway or see her after school. She and I weren't in any classes together so it didn't happen too often, and our interactions were usually brief. I'd mutter something childish like, "Hi, how's it going," while Sophia smiled and greeted me by name. I loved that she remembered my name. She was one of the few who did.

Victor and I didn't have any classes together either, so the only time we talked was before or after school. On days when he was absent, I had no clue what to do with myself. It was an odd feeling to be surrounded by people and still feel so alone. But honestly I didn't think about it much. I'd grown so used to being on my own, it didn't bother me. Not in any way I noticed at the time. I did what I had to do. I went to school. I didn't get in trouble. I kept the family rules. And I tried my hardest to make sure I wasn't a burden on anyone. In a way I felt more comfortable being overlooked. Ghost-like.

It was Friday afternoon before Halloween and all the kids at school were about to explode with excitement as we waited for the bell to ring that afternoon. The entire week had been filled with chatter about everyone's plans for the weekend. Party invitations were everywhere, floating around the school like confetti during a parade. There were at least half a dozen parties I'd heard about, and although I knew countless details about each of them, I hadn't been invited to any. I didn't think Victor had been either, but I wasn't sure because he was absent that day. Tonsillitis. It was something particularly tough for Victor since it hindered his ability to speak. One of his favorite pastimes. Somehow we all managed to make it to the final bell that day without imploding, and with literal shouts of glee, everyone raced out of the building and onto their weekend plans. Plans consisting of candy, costumes, and fun.

I made my way out of the school and was sitting on the concrete steps near the carpool line waiting for Mrs. Cooper to pick me up. Usually Victor would be there with me rambling on and on about anything that popped into his brain, but that day I sat alone. Students raced off in all directions, and I wondered how it would feel to be one of them. To have their lives. To have friends and a real family. A family that was there no matter what. One with a real mom and dad who cared about me and thought of me as their own. I usually tried not to think about things like that. Those type of thoughts never helped change anything. My life was mine and wishing it was different wouldn't make any difference.

I had nearly finished off the cookie left over from lunch when I was startled by a hand on my shoulder and a kind voice. "Hey, Chase. Do you care if I sit with you for a minute?" It was Sophia. Out of instinct I glanced around to make sure it was actually me she meant to speak to. I suppose the fact that she said my name should have given it away.

"Sure," I said as I tossed the last bite of cookie aside.

Sophia sat right next to me and smirked like she could tell how awkward I felt. "We haven't talked in forever. How have you been?"

"I'm good…I guess." I wanted to say more. To have a real conversation, but Sophia made me nervous. Somehow her presence made it difficult for words to find their way from my brain to my mouth.

"Do you have any big plans this weekend?" she said.

"Umm…not really. I'll probably just stay home or whatever."

"Stay home? You can't do that. It's Halloween. You have to go out. Get some candy and have fun."

"I guess I'm just not that into Halloween." It was a total lie. Halloween was the best. I just didn't want to look like the loser who had no friends.

"Well, that stinks," Sophia said as she stared off toward the parking lot. "I was going to ask if you wanted to come to my house this weekend. I'm having a party Saturday."

"Oh really?" I said, trying my best not to act excited.

"Yeah, I think it would be great if you'd come. You can bring Victor too."

"I'll think about it," I said. "Sounds like fun." That was partially true. I wanted to be there so I could spend more time around Sophia. But I had no desire to be around most of the other kids in our grade. "Who all is going to be there?"

"Just some friends," Sophia said. She turned her eyes back to me and smiled. "Don't worry; I didn't invite any jerks."

"So a 'no jerks allowed' party?"

"That's right. And trust me, that doesn't leave very many people to choose from. You should be happy. You made the cut." Sophia and I laughed as her mom pulled up and waved from the carpool line. "See you later, Chase," she said as she raced away. "You better be there."

I did show up that night. Stood right there in front of Sophia's house like I did the night Ember was with me. I could hear kids in the backyard giggling and squealing over the thud of music. Victor hadn't recovered, so I was by myself. Standing. Waiting. What I was waiting for, I'm not sure. But it never came. I often wondered why I didn't join the party that night. I wasn't comfortable going and I wasn't comfortable not going. One piece of me was fighting to make sure I put myself out there. To be a part. To be happy. But the other piece of me was fighting to stay protected. To play it safe. To never get hurt. To be alone.

"Alright, talk," Ember said to Echo as we ducked inside my tent.

"Relax, Ember," I said as she huffed at me. "What's going on, Echo? What did you want to tell us?" Echo was a wreck. He was sweating, wringing his hands, and his eyes were blinking at hyper-speed while he scanned the room like he thought someone else might be there. "Echo, are you okay?"

"I - I want to tell you something, b - but I'm not supposed to," Echo managed to get out.

"Okay, is it important?" I said. Echo nodded. "Is it about what happened to Setu or Cedric?"

"Yes," he said. "Both." His eyes stilled and he honed in on me. "And s - something about you."

"Something about me? What is it? Am I in danger?"

Ember couldn't hold it in anymore. "Just spit it out, Echo. There's no one here but us. No one will know anything you tell us."

"Let's start with Setu," I said hoping to calm him down. "Where did The Collector send him? Is he okay?"

"The Collector...he's upset," Echo began. "Something went wrong. He sent a message to Analise and Olivia telling them to find out what happened."

Ember motioned for us to take a seat on the floor. Echo was a bit reluctant, but finally sat. It seemed like one wrong word or loud noise might cause him to bolt. "Did something go wrong:" Ember asked. "Did something happen to Setu?"

"No - I - I mean yes," Echo said as he rubbed his hands

on his pant legs. "It's both of them. Setu and Cedric. He can't find them."

"The Collector?" I said. Echo nodded. "He has to know where he sent them. Why can't he find them?" I hoped he would relax enough to be able to fill in the gaps of his story.

"They aren't where they're supposed to be," he went on. He took a deep breath and his eyes grew wide. "Somehow, he lost them. And he's really mad about it. He has all of our Seers working on it, and he's demanding they let him know something immediately. He's worried another group is interfering."

"Another group?" Ember said. "You mean a group like us? Another circus?"

"I don't think it's a circus," Echo said. His voice shook a little less than before and his hands weren't fidgeting so much. "But it is a group with abilities. He said they're dangerous and we need to find out as much as we can about them."

I looked at Ember who seemed to be just as confused as I was. Thoughts swirled inside my head and I tried to capture them and order them into a sentence. "I know The Collector talks a lot about there being danger out there," I said. "He always tells us he's working to protect us from it, but I never thought he meant something like this."

"And why would some other group care what we do?" Ember said. "We're just a circus."

"It isn't us they care about," Echo said. There was a steadiness to his voice. He was composed and intense. "It's The Collector. He said they wanted to interfere with his work.

I don't think he meant the circus. I think something else is going on."

Ember's forehead wrinkled and her eyes moved around the room as her mind searched for answers. "Do you have any idea what kind of work he's talking about? Is it searching for people with abilities? Collecting them?"

"I'm not sure," Echo said. "But I don't think that's it either. He told Analise that he was close. That he could feel it."

"Do you think he was talking about me?" I said. "About me discovering my ability?"

"I *know* he was talking about you," Echo said dropping his eyes. "I didn't want to say anything. I made a vow that I'd never leak information. But I can't help it." Echo's eyes filled with tears and his hands were shaking.

"It's okay, Echo," I said. "We'll keep anything you tell us a secret. We're your friends."

Echo wiped at his eyes and composed himself enough to speak clearly. "The Collector — he needs you. Or, he needs your ability anyway. He's tired of waiting for you to manifest. He has a plan to force it out of you. I don't know exactly how, but I know it's supposed to happen before the end of the week."

"We're only here for two more days," Ember said. "Do you have any idea what he has planned?"

"He never said," Echo replied. "But I know it involves Luka."

"What does Luka have to do with it?" Ember said. "Luka's just a bodyguard."

"He's more than a bodyguard," Echo said. "I know

everyone thinks he has the ability of strength, but that's not true. His ability is very rare. He's powerful."

"What is it, Echo?" I said. "What's his ability?"

Echo nervously cleared his throat. "Luka is a Reaper."

"A Reaper?" Ember said barely above a whisper. "I thought those were made up. I didn't know Reapers were real."

"Wait, what's a Reaper?" I asked. I'd never heard the word used in the circus, but by the sound of it, I assumed it wasn't good.

Echo attempted to explain. "A Reaper is someone who — you know when like there's a flower and if you touch it too much — or like when you have a fish when you're a kid and you want to pet it but your parents won't let you — It's like he —"

"He kills things," Ember said flatly. "With just a touch he can hurt or kill any living thing. He can stop the blood in your veins, trap the air in your lungs, or fill your body with tumors. All with a touch. He's basically...death in human form."

Hearing those words, it was as if Luka had stopped my heart without even coming close to me. The thought of a person being so powerful was terrifying. If what Echo said was true, The Collector was going to force my ability out of me and Luka would be the tool he used. And even though I didn't know exactly how it would play out, I knew it wouldn't be pleasant. I instantly felt sick and thought I might throw up. Ember must have noticed because she placed a hand on my back. "Don't worry, Chase," she said. "I won't let anything like that happen to you. Luka isn't the only one around here who's powerful."

"I wouldn't talk like that if I were you," Echo said. "Words like that could be considered treasonous."

"Treason or not, no one hurts my friends."

"It's okay, Ember," I said. It wasn't okay, but I didn't want Ember to do anything she might regret. "We don't know what's happening yet."

Ember threw her hands up and groaned. "So we're supposed to wait and find out? We're just gonna sit around and hope nothing bad happens?"

"I think that's all we can do. For now."

Echo spoke up. "I'll see if there's anything else I can find."

"And I have a session with Olivia today," I said. "I'll see if I can get anything out of her."

Ember sighed. "I guess I'll just snoop around then."

"Be careful, Ember," I said. "You too, Echo. We can't afford to make a mistake. I don't want to see any of us end up Forsaken." They both nodded in agreement. "We'll get together later and share what we find out."

"Sounds good," Ember said. She paused for a moment and turned her gaze to Echo. "Thanks, Echo. I know this wasn't easy for you. Thanks for giving us a heads up on all of this. We owe you one."

Echo stood up and dusted his pants off. "You're welcome," he said. "But you don't owe me anything. Friends look out for each other, right?"

Ember smiled. "That's right."

Echo turned to leave but stopped and looked back. "Interesting fact…Did you know researchers have discovered that certain species of animals actually form and maintain friendships?"

"Is he serious right now?" Ember said.

"For example, primates obviously have more complex relationships, but also elephants and dolphins have been know to —"

"Thanks Echo," Ember said as she jumped up and walked him out. "Let us know if you find anything."

When Echo was gone, Ember turned and looked at me in a way I'd never forget. Her eyes were like stone and her face was firm and set. And when she spoke, it sounded more like she was making a vow. Promising something she would do even if it cost her everything. "I mean it, Chase. I won't let them hurt you. Luka, Analise, The Collector…I don't care who it is. If they try to hurt you, they'll pay."

I wanted to tell her not to say such things. That she shouldn't even have thoughts like that. That she didn't have to be concerned with protecting me. But truthfully, I was glad Ember was on my side. I also knew that it didn't matter what I said to her, Ember made her own decisions.

CHAPTER FOURTEEN

OLIVIA WAS MORE anxious than usual. I stepped into her office and found her shuffling through papers like she had misplaced a top secret document. She didn't notice me at first. She simply went about her searching, mumbling to herself. I didn't catch everything Olivia said, but she was muttering something about time running short and how this was a bad idea. I cleared my throat which startled her. She quickly composed herself and hid her anxiety with the phoniest smile I'd ever seen. "Come in, Chase," she said. Her weak smile promptly faded and unmistakable concern returned to her razor-like face. "Are you ready to begin?"

"I am," I said as I took my seat. "Is everything okay?"

Olivia didn't answer immediately. She took her time gathering her things before sitting in the chair across from me. Her silence only stoked my anxiety. "I'm fine. Things are just a little tense right now."

"Anything I need to be worried about?" I wanted to pry, but I couldn't risk upsetting her. I had to chose my words carefully.

"Nothing we can't work through," Olivia said. She paused and scribbled something on her notepad. "I want to try something a little different today." I nodded and tried to get a look at what she wrote. I couldn't make it out. Olivia turned the notepad upside down. "Alright, Chase. Close your eyes and try to relax."

Just as always, the moment Olivia pressed her finger against my forehead, I was freed from my present thoughts and felt as if I was floating in a sea of memories. That time was different though because I never seemed to settle anywhere. Typically, Olivia would take my mind to a very specific point in time and I'd arrive as quickly as blinking my eyes. But for some reason I couldn't gain my bearings. Pictures zipped in and out of my consciousness like a filmstrip, flashing and skipping scenes. Homes and faces, lakes and mountains and fields of grass, bedrooms and classrooms, old men and newborn babies. They all swirled around at dizzying speeds, sights and sounds pressing in on me, each of them fighting for space. Then, all at once, everything went black. I sat still for a moment, hoping Olivia hadn't lost or forgotten me. A single light bulb flickered to life above me, illuminating a narrow, stark white hallway. The floor, the ceiling, and the walls, were all gleaming white. Spotless.

"Are you there, Chase?" Olivia called to me. She seemed far away, a faint voice in the distance.

"I'm here," I answered. "Only I don't know where *here is*."

"Move forward."

With a bit of hesitation, I took a couple of steps when another light bulb blinked on. I continued moving down the hallway, one step in front of the other, and every few steps another light flickered on to light the space directly in front of me. "Where am I?"

"You'll see soon," Olivia said. Her voice drew nearer as I walked. The hallway seemed to stretch on for miles as I continued to move ahead one step at a time. I couldn't help but wonder if this was some sort of test or cruel punishment. But, ultimately, I came to a dead end and stood facing a seamless white door with a bright gold doorknob. "Go ahead," Olivia said. "Step inside."

I turned the knob and pushed against the heavy door. As soon as I stepped inside, it shut behind me with a heavy thud. The room was round, without windows, and was perfectly white just like the hallway. A golden chandelier hung from the center of the ceiling. It resembled a tangled mass of shiny deer antlers, and it lit up the room with warm streaks of light that cast thin gray shadows in all directions. Directly under the chandelier, sat two small chairs. One of them was empty, and in the other sat Olivia. "I'm glad you made it, Chase," she said. She spoke softly, but her voice boomed through the utter silence of that room. "Please…sit."

I slowly inched toward the chair. "What is this?" I asked as I eased into my seat. "Where am I?"

"Don't worry, you're safe here. This place may seem unfamiliar but I assure you it all came from you."

"I don't have any memory of this. Have I been here before?"

"No," Olivia said. "The hallway and this room are bits and pieces I took from some of your previous memories. I combined everything and created this space for you. For us. So we can talk."

"I didn't know you could do that," I said. "I thought

you could only see what I see. I didn't know you could...
create things."

"Our abilities are seldom one-dimensional. There are
always skills to learn and variances to discover."

I took another look around the room, searching for
something familiar. "So what is all of this about? Why are
we here?"

Olivia sat up straight and took a deep breath. "I apologize
for the secrecy, but I had to make sure no one overheard us."
She motioned to the area around us. "This place...this room
was taken from your memories. I can see you and speak to
you without fear of being discovered."

"Why do we need privacy? Is something wrong? Am I
in danger?"

Olivia placed her hands in her lap. "Yes, Chase, you are
in danger. I'm sorry to be so blunt, but I've come to warn
you and hopefully help you. But if I am going to help you,
I need all the information I can get. I have some questions
to ask you, and I need you to be honest."

"I understand," I said hesitantly. "I'll tell you what I can,
but I have some questions too."

"What is it you want to know?" Olivia said, eyebrows
raised. She was gravely serious, but there was sincerity in
her words.

"Is The Collector planning on doing something to force
my ability out of me?"

Olivia stared at me over the rim of her glasses. "Yes, he
is."

"Do you know how he plans to do it?"

"No, not exactly. I do know that many of us discover our

abilities as a result of a tragic or disturbing event. I believe he intends to create such an event in hopes that your ability will manifest."

"And that's supposed to happen soon?"

"Not if we act," Olivia said.

"Why would he do something like that? Why would he want to hurt me? I thought The Collector loved us — that we were his family."

Olivia wrung her hands, stared at the chandelier — then back at me. "I believe he does love you. And he does consider you family. But The Collector is driven by something else... something bigger. He sees this as a necessity. He doesn't want to hurt you. But he will."

Echo's words were still fresh on my mind. I had to find out how much truth there was in what he told me. "What is so important to him that he's willing to hurt me to get it?"

"That's not for me to say. All I can tell you is, I've followed The Collector for many years. I have always been an obedient servant. But I don't agree with him on this. It's cruel to force a manifest. I want to avoid it if at all possible."

"How do we do that?"

"First, my questions," Olivia said flatly. "Have you been visited by anyone?"

"Visited?"

"Yes, whether in your mind or in person. Have you spoken to anyone outside of the circus? Anyone who seemed to know you?"

"I haven't talked to anyone other than my friend Sophia. That was when The Collector gave Ember and me a pass earlier this week."

"Have you seen anyone unusual?" she asked. "Someone who seems out of place or anyone snooping around the circus?"

Immediately, he came to mind. "There was one man," I said. "I've seen him on the grounds a couple of times now, but I never talked to him."

Olivia snatched up her legal pad and began scribbling notes. "Tell me about him. Describe him. Tell me what he did and what made you notice him."

Her sharp tone and the way she slid to the edge of her seat, made it clear the information was important. "Well, he was an average guy, kind of thin with short dark hair. He was wearing khaki pants, a white shirt, and a bright green bow tie."

"And he stood out to you? Like he didn't belong here?"

"Yes. Both times I saw him, he looked directly at me. I know it sounds weird, but it was like he was watching me. He was there one second and gone the next. I even chased him the last time I saw him, but he got away."

"And you never reported this?" Olivia said, glaring at me over her glasses again. "You never let anyone know?"

"No, I didn't," I said. "I know I should have, but I didn't. I can't explain it. It's like I knew reporting it was the right thing to do, but my mind shut those thoughts out. I don't know if that makes sense."

"When something like that happens, you have to report it, Chase," Olivia said as she sat back in her seat. "There are people out there with powers like ours. They are dangerous, and The Collector has to know if anything unusual happens."

"I know. I'm sorry."

Olivia huffed in an attempt to smother her disappointment. "I suppose what's done is done. But, I need to hear everything. Every detail. Go back to the first time you saw him and let me know everything that was happening, everything you saw, everything you felt. It's all very important."

I spent the next few minutes recounting every detail I could remember though most of it seemed meaningless. There wasn't much to tell. I'd only seen him twice for a few brief moments. A vague description was about all I had to offer. When I finished, Olivia wrote her last sentence and sat there in silence for a moment, staring at her papers. "Is there anything…anything I can do?" I asked. The words felt strange leaving my mouth, but I needed an answer. Learning that Olivia didn't agree with The Collector's idea of forcing my ability from me was uncomfortable enough. Hearing that she wanted to stop him was grounds for becoming Forsaken. Even mentioning such things could get her in serious trouble.

"Let's hope it doesn't come to you having to *do* anything," Olivia said somberly. "If things progress to that end, we're both in trouble."

I nodded. "I understand." Surprisingly, Olivia looked at me with caring eyes. It was something I'd never seen from her. I thought it might be a good opportunity to learn something more. "Can you tell me what he thinks my ability is? Or why he needs me so badly."

"I wish I could," Olivia said. "It's never good for an Evo to have an idea of his ability before it manifests. Knowing can interfere with the process. Knowing often results in the Evo trying to make something specific happen. And truthfully, no one can know your ability for certain until it shows itself."

"But he needs me," I said. "My ability, I mean."

Olivia nodded sharply. "He does."

"What is it that's so important? There are so many powerful people here already. What could The Collector possibly need from me?"

Olivia set her pad and pen on the floor beside her once again before placing her hands in her lap. "Chase, it won't be long before you learn some things about The Collector. Despite what you may hear, I want you to know something. The Collector is a good man. He isn't perfect. Then again, none of us is. But he is good. Some things in life are difficult to deal with under normal circumstances. When you have abilities like his, things can be especially difficult."

"It seems like having the ability to travel through time would make things easy to deal with. If something goes wrong, you can just go back and correct it. You can go back as many times as you need to make things right."

"It would seem that way," Olivia said. "But it doesn't work like that. It's not so simple."

"I don't understand."

"Traveling through time and space, when you have the ability to do so, can be simple in concept. However, *changing* things that happen in the past in an attempt to alter the future, is much trickier and sometimes downright impossible."

"So there is something in the past that The Collector can't change? And he thinks my ability might help him change it?"

Olivia smirked. "You're a smart young man, Chase. You're right. There's something from The Collector's past he desperately wants to change, but he can't do so through his ability alone. He needs someone else. He believes that person is you."

"I don't see what he could need from me."

"I know," Olivia said. "You will soon enough."

"Why is there such a rush to make it happen?"

"The Collector is…running out of time. The window for altering his circumstances is quickly closing. He's become obsessed with you and your ability. He needs you to manifest. He needs it to happen now."

"How can he be running out of time? He controls time."

"No one controls time."

"But The Collector —"

"The Collector travels through time. He experiences time. He uses it as a tool to assist him in reaching his goals. But make no mistake, Chase…time cannot be controlled. Time marches forward regardless of our silly games or grandiose plans. Time conquers us all. It will keep going long after you and I are gone, and it will continue to press on even when The Collector and his circus are no more."

"If The Collector is so desperate for me to discover my ability, and if he's running out of time, then how can you stop him?"

"For now, I'm trying to reason with him. As I told you, he's an honorable man. His heart is good. I just need him to see the damage that forcing your ability out of you could do, not only to you, but to his ultimate goal."

"And if he won't listen to reason?"

Olivia hesitated, her eyes cut from side to side. "I suppose we'll make that decision when and if the time comes. Just be ready."

"Ready for what exactly?"

"Ready for anything." She paused. "One more thing, Chase. You obviously know more than you should about all of this. Where did you get your information?"

It was the question I was hoping she wouldn't ask. I knew too much, and I was careless for letting her realize it. "I… don't know if I should say."

Olivia removed her glasses and leaned forward. "Chase, we are both in this now. There are things you mentioned that are impossible for you to know unless someone told you. It has to be someone with access to sensitive information. I'm not trying to catch anyone, and I certainly can't turn in that person for sharing it with you. You and I…we have to trust one another. If there's someone else I can trust, that would be very helpful in keeping you safe."

Against my better judgment, I cleared my throat and said the very thing I intended to keep secret. "It was Echo. He told me everything. Ember and me. But I promised him I wouldn't tell anyone."

Olivia smiled and nodded. "That makes perfect sense," she said. "You have loyal friends."

Without another word, Olivia reached out and pressed her finger against my forehead and I instantly woke up. I was sitting in her office as usual as she puttered around behind her desk. "Oh, there you are," she said as she organized her things. "Good to have you back."

I was a little woozy still, but the hazy feeling was fading quickly. "Olivia, what we talked about. Is is okay if —"

"What we talked about?" she said. "I don't know what you mean?"

"Just a second ago," I said. "When we were in the white —"

"You're probably experiencing a little confusion brought on by the lengthy session we had today. You may feel a bit off for a while, but the disorientation will pass soon. Drink plenty of water and…" She paused.

"Yeah?"

"Try not to worry. Everything will work out."

I left Olivia's office feeling more stressed than when I'd gone in. I'd learned a little about The Collector, but only enough to spark more questions. I wanted to ask Olivia if it was okay for me to tell Ember and Echo about our talk. However, by the way she avoided the subject, it was clear the conversation wasn't something she was even willing to admit happened. So, since they were my friends, I told them everything. Ember was shocked and a little angry about the confirmation that The Collector wanted to force my ability from me. Echo was uncomfortable and didn't say much. I didn't tell him I told Olivia he'd given me the information. I didn't want to worry him. We went our separate ways that night and I tossed around in my cot until I finally fell asleep. I was restless and worried about what might happen soon, but mostly I was scared. I was afraid the events of the next day or two would rip me from the family I'd built at the circus. Becoming a Forsaken and being dropped off somewhere in time, didn't concern me nearly as much as being permanently separated from those I loved. My friends.

CHAPTER FIFTEEN

"STEP INTO THE hallway, Chase," Mrs. Chase said. I had been caught in a shoving match with a Robbie Frazier who'd pointed out to the class that I failed my spelling test. He was always doing things like that. Looking for ways to make fun of others or make himself look smarter. Truthfully, I failed because I was up all night with Jeremy, the kid I shared a room with in my new home. He was a few years older than me and spent most days angry about something. I had gotten used to his outbursts, but that night he was especially over the top. Jeremy was set off after he got caught at dinner trying to sneak ravioli into a napkin. He hated ravioli and hoped to toss it in the trash without being seen. I honestly didn't think it was that big of a deal, but for some reason he blew up. He ranted and yelled and screamed and threw things most of the night. I wasn't able to think let alone study. So I failed my test, and Robbie wanted everyone to know. I lost my cool and pushed him. He pushed back. It got out of hand. Intense fourth grade drama.

"I'm sorry, Mrs. Chase," I said as she shut the classroom door behind us. I wasn't sorry, but I also didn't want trouble. "Robbie started it. If he would have kept his big mouth shut, nothing would have happened."

Mrs. Chase didn't answer immediately. She took her time, staring down at me like she was searching for what to say. The pause was painful. Much worse than if she would've just yelled at me. "Chase, you know I can't have students pushing and shoving when they get angry."

"I know, but Robbie —"

"Robbie, said things you didn't want to hear. He was rude and he embarrassed you in front of your classmates. Is that right?"

"Yes," I answered.

"And when he embarrassed you, it made you angry? And because you were angry, you decided to push him?"

"Yes." I felt tears beginning to well up. Partly because I didn't want to disappoint Mrs. Chase and partly because I was still mad. "But now everyone thinks I'm stupid. I'm not stupid; I just had a bad — I was up all night because my dumb roommate was throwing things around the room and yelling about how —"

"Chase, I understand." Mrs. Chase said, placing a hand on my shoulder. Her eyes were kind and her words were softer than I expected. She lowered herself to one knee and looked me right in the eye. Her words were burned into my memory. "Everyone has problems, Chase. I do. Jeremy does. Robbie does. You do too. Just because you have problems in your life, it doesn't mean you can use that as a reason to mistreat others. I believe you know that. And I know you're better than that."

It was still dark out the next morning when I awoke suddenly with a knot in my chest. I laid still for a moment, listening, trying to figure out what was happening that had me so shaken. My anxiety was through the roof. I was sweating and breathing heavily, and my fists were clinched. I felt ridiculous since nothing was *really* wrong. No one was after me. Nothing bad was happening. There was only silence and the thudding of my heart. I held still on my cot, trying to force myself to calm down. Relax. It didn't work. I sat up, hoping a deep breath of cool night air might help when suddenly the voice of a man spoke to me. Sitting there in my tent, at the foot of my bed, was the man with the green bow tie.

"What are you doing here?" I yelped as I jumped from my cot.

He held up both hands, mouth and eyes fully opened. "Wait. I didn't mean to scare you. It's okay. You're okay. I'm not here to hurt you. I only want to talk."

It was the first time I'd heard the man speak. He seemed genuine even though it was kind of disturbing that he was sitting in my tent while I slept. "So talk," I said in my most forceful tone. "Who are you, and what do you want?"

"My name is Jackson. I'm a messenger."

"A messenger?"

"Well, more like a spy actually, but tonight I'm a messenger. I'm here to help. To warn you."

"Warn me about what? About creeps sneaking into my tent?"

Jackson tilted his head to the side. "Fair enough, but no. I'm definitely here to help."

"You have ten seconds before I wake up this whole circus."

"Oh, please don't do that," Jackson said, pressing his hands together. "That would simply ruin everything."

"Ten...nine...eight..."

"Okay, okay...I'm here to prepare you. Tomorrow, something is going to happen. Something terrible. I need to make sure you're safe and that you're ready."

He had my attention. It was the second time in as many days that someone had told me to be ready. "Ready for what exactly?"

Jackson cleared his throat and adjusted his tie. He was younger than I originally thought. Probably just a few years older than I was. "Well...you need to be ready to go. We're getting you out of here."

"Who exactly is 'we,' and why would I go anywhere with you?"

"It's simple really," Jackson said. "We're people like you. People with abilities. You call yourselves The Lost. We are known as The Unseen. I was sent here to warn you. And to rescue you, of course."

"I don't need rescuing, and I'm not going anywhere."

"Give me a second to explain. Your leader — The Collector, or whatever he's calling himself now — he's not a good person. I know he talks a great game about being a family and caring about everyone, but it's all misleading. The truth is, he wants what you have and he'll hurt you to get it."

"I'm just supposed to take your word for it? I don't even know who you are. You sneak in here in the middle of the night and expect me to believe everything you say? You want me to leave here, and just hope you're telling me the truth?"

"No, that's not how it works."

"Then tell me how it works because this is my family. I have friends here. I can't just leave."

"Shh…" Jackson said, holding up his hands again and cutting his eyes toward the entrance of the tent. "Please, keep it down. I only want to help you. I'd never expect you to *take my word for it.* This is far too important for something like that. You need to see for yourself." Jackson reached into his pocket and pulled out a small purple stone. It shimmered in the dim moonlight and hummed with energy. "Pretty, isn't it?"

"What is that?"

"It's a memory stone."

"I've never heard of that. What is a memory stone?"

Jackson pursed his lips and thought for a moment. "You know how you have sessions with Olivia?"

"The ones where she reads my thoughts?"

"Not your thoughts…your memories."

"Right," I said. "That's what I meant."

"Well the memory stone is like a recording device. Olivia probably has quite a few of them hidden away somewhere. Anytime a memory is read, it can be recorded on a stone."

"So there's a memory on there? One you want me to see?"

"Yes, and I think it will answer some questions for you."

"How does it work? I'm guessing you can't just press play."

"Not quite," Jackson said, twirling the stone in his fingers. "I touch it to your forehead. The same way Olivia does when she does a reading for you. Since she's a Seer, she can accomplish the same result with her finger. Unfortunately, I am not a Seer, so I brought the stone."

"I'm not touching that thing," I said. "No offense, but

I don't know you, and I don't trust you. And since we're the only two around, there's no way —"

"Morning, gentlemen," Ember said as she stepped into the tent. Jackson immediately leaped to his feet and backed away, pressing into the side of the tent. "Is everything okay, Chase?" Her eyes were locked onto Jackson in a deadly stare as if she wanted nothing more than to incinerate him.

"Now t-t-take it easy," Jackson muttered. "There's no need to get upset."

Both of Ember's hands ignited into a bright red flame. "Upset?" she said blankly. "I'm not upset. Not unless I need to be. Chase? Do I need to be?"

"Everything is good, Ember," I said. "This is Jackson. He's here to tell me —"

"I know why he's here," Ember said. "I heard everything. I was keeping an eye out since so many weird things have been happening. Good thing I was around."

Ember's hands were still aflame, and her eyes were still fixed on Jackson who was beginning to cower. "Ember," I said. "It's okay. Let's hear him out."

"Fine," Ember said. With a puff of smoke, the fire was extinguished and Ember's hands returned to normal. "Let's talk, Jackson. First of all, why are you here?"

Jackson stumbled back to the chair and took a seat. "Well, like I said, I'm here to warn —"

"No," Ember cut in. "I'm asking why this is so important to you. To your people. What are you called again? The Unfound or something?"

"The Unseen," Jackson said, clearing his throat. "And I'm not authorized to reveal the nature of our mission."

"Is that right?" Ember said. "Well, you're not authorized to be in this circus either, but here you are. So you can either talk, or I can turn you over to The Collector. *Or* I could fry you like a piece of chicken."

I tried to speak up. To stop Ember from saying anymore threatening comments, but Jackson spoke first. "It's okay, Chase. It's a fair question." He paused for a moment and fiddled with his bow tie. "You see, there are certain…rules for people with abilities. Ones that must be followed."

"No one has ever told us about any rules," I said. "Not outside the ones we have in the circus anyway."

"That isn't surprising," Jackson said. "The Collector keeps you cut off from any others with abilities. It's a way for him to maintain control. He makes the rules for you. Ones he requires to keep things running smoothly. But there are rules bigger than the circus — bigger than The Collector. Rules that all people with abilities must keep. The Collector is aware of that. He knows he has broken several longstanding rules. He'll have to be held accountable."

"Exactly which rules did he break?" Ember asked.

"Well, for one, he keeps you all from leaving," Jackson said.

"That's for our protection," Ember said. "He told us there are dangerous people who want to hurt us."

"That may be true. But holding you here…keeping you locked away from the rest of the world. He can't do that."

"We aren't forced to stay," I said. "We can leave if we want. We're told that from day one. The Collector wants us to be safe."

"Very well," Jackson said. "But unfortunately that's only

the beginning. The Collector is also guilty of using his gifts for personal gain. Everyone does that to some extent, usually in a monetary sense, but his ability is extremely powerful. Abusing an ability to bend time and space can put the entire world at risk. Especially when it's used for his own benefit. Think about it. He takes people. Snatches them from their homes and infuses them into his world to grow his circus. His collection."

"Not everyone here was snatched from their homes," I said. "Some of us are glad to be here. Most of us are happy to be a part of the circus." I glanced at Ember, but she didn't make eye contact. She simply lowered her head.

"That may be true for you," Jackson continued. "But it's not true for everyone." He paused. "Tell me Chase, when someone makes a mistake or breaks one of The Collector's rules, what happens to them?" I didn't answer. I didn't want to answer. "He banishes them. He drops them off somewhere in time to be lost forever. That cannot be allowed to continue."

"So why now?" Ember said. "This has been going on for years, but as soon as it involves Chase, you want to do something about it? What's so different now?"

"That's exactly why I brought this," Jackson said, holding up the glowing memory stone. "This is one of The Collectors memories. If you'll just watch it, I think you'll understand."

"We're not touching that thing," Ember said. "Just tell us what the memory is."

"I'm not allowed to tell you any details. I am only authorized to show you."

Ember huffed. "And I don't allow my friends to touch strange, enchanted objects carried around by people who sneak into tents at night." Ember held up her right hand, igniting it in a show of intimidation. "So, talk."

"You don't understand," Jackson said. "I can't talk about it." He turned his head and pulled his shirt collar down to reveal a mark similar to the ones Analise had given us. His was slightly different. It was a circle with a smaller solid black circle inside of it. A thin line divided the entire mark. "I haven't seen the memory on the stone and even if I had, this mark prevents me from sharing any details concerning The Collector's crimes. In fact, the stone was *supposed* to be for Chase's eyes only, but as you know, that didn't go as planned."

"Then you'll have to find another way to convince us you're telling the truth," Ember said.

"Olivia told me The Collector had things going on in his life that were difficult to deal with," I said. "Does that memory have something to do with what's happening?"

Jackson nodded. "The Collector is grieving, Chase. He's grieving in a way you or I could never understand. That grief is clouding his judgment."

"Grieving? How?" Ember said. "And how is Chase supposed to do anything about that?"

Jackson shrugged and pointed to the mark on his neck. "I'm sorry. I suppose you'll have to trust me until I can get you to Ms. Genevieve. She will answer all of your questions."

"Maybe you don't understand," Ember said. "We're not going anywhere with you. And whoever this Ms. Genevieve is, she can come to us if she wants to talk."

"Listen, maybe there's something I can do," Jackson said, sliding a little closer to us. "If I tell you what's going to happen tomorrow, will you believe I'm telling you the truth?"

"It's a start," I said. "What's supposed to happen?"

"It's not what's *supposed* to happen," Jackson said. "It's what will happen. It's certain. Ms. Genevieve has seen it."

"No one can read the future," Ember said. "The future isn't written. Even The Collector doesn't know. He can only take the circus as far as the present. If he can't do it —"

"Ms. Genevieve is far more powerful than The Collector," Jackson said. "And what you're saying is mostly true. The future is unwritten, and no one is capable of traveling there to experience it. But Ms. Genevieve can see glimpses. She's seen how this plays out, and she knows what will happen tomorrow. Let us help you. If I tell you what's going to happen — if it really does happen, will you believe me?"

"I don't know," Ember said. "Spill it."

Jackson rubbed his hands together and spoke quickly like he wanted to get it all out before we changed our minds. "Regardless of what I'm about to tell you, you need to go about your day as normally as possible tomorrow. If The Collector has any hint that something out of the ordinary is happening, he'll change his plan and we'll be going in blind. Chase, this may be difficult to hear, but his plan is to harm someone you care about."

"I thought his plan was to harm me," I said.

"It is, in a way. He hopes by putting them in mortal danger, he'll force you into manifesting. The idea is your instincts will override everything else. You'll manifest in order to help them."

I glanced at Ember. "Who is it? Who will he try to hurt?"

"That is unclear. Ms. Genevieve said the individual was veiled in shadow. She believes it's because The Collector hasn't decided yet."

"So it could be me?" Ember said.

"Yes," Jackson said somberly. "I'm sorry, Ember, but it could very well be you or your friend Echo."

"What exactly is he planning to do?" I said.

"Are you familiar with Luka?" Jackson asked.

"We know Luka," Ember said. "He's The Collector's bodyguard. He and Analise are never far away from him."

Up to that point, everything Jackson told was lined up with what Echo shared, but I still wanted to test how much he know. "Rumor is Luka has the ability of strength, but that's just because of his size. No one knows for sure."

"It's not strength that makes Luka so valuable to The Collector," Jackson said. "It's much worse. Luka is a Reaper."

"We already know about The Collector's plan and that it involves Luka," Ember said.

Jackson went on. "Did you know he plans to make this some sort of public spectacle? Ms. Genevieve said she saw all eyes on Luka and the one The Collector chooses."

"We have a good idea," Ember said. "It's how he usually handles things."

"Did you know it happens tomorrow?" Jackson let those words hang for a moment. I think he wanted us to realize how badly we needed him. "That's why I'm here. There's a plan to get you out. To take you away from here and to keep The Collector from using you."

"What if I don't want to be...taken?" I said.

"The Collector needs to be stopped, and you are the key to doing so," Jackson said. "If all goes well, we'll reunite you with your friends when the time comes."

"I can't just leave," I said, even though the words sounded

a bit ridiculous. "I can't leave Ember and Echo. They're my friends."

Jackson nodded and exhaled a deep breath. "I hear your concern, Chase, but you have to understand…some things are bigger than our friendships. Some things are are more important than being with those we care about."

"If he goes, I go," Ember said. "And Echo too."

Jackson dropped his head. "I'll see what I can do. But I can't promise."

"Personally, I don't think it'll come to that," Ember went on. "No one is going to hurt me, Echo, or Chase. I'll do whatever it takes to make sure that doesn't happen."

"I sincerely hope you're right," Jackson said. "But for now, I have to go. They're expecting me back." He stood and moved toward the exit. "Remember, be careful and go about your day as if it was any other day. And good luck." Jackson was halfway out of the tent when he stopped and looked back. "Oh, and here." He tossed the memory stone to me, and I caught the glowing rock. It was warm and the skin on my hand tingled a bit at its touch. "You keep that, and use it if you want. Just touch it to your forehead." Jackson ducked out of the tent, leaving Ember and me staring at one another. It was impossible to know what was going to happen, but we had a sickening feeling it would change everything for us.

CHAPTER SIXTEEN

WHETHER OR NOT we could trust Jackson was yet to be seen, but I figured it couldn't hurt for Ember and me to carry on with our day as normal. It was the last evening the circus would be in town, and luckily my last day cleaning animal stalls. Zuki met me before sunrise and was as irritable as usual. The only time she smiled that morning was when she asked if "Fire Girl" would be stopping by. I shrugged and Zuki grunted and pushed a shovel into my hand. Lack of sleep had me feeling exhausted and slightly nauseous, but all I could think about was what the day might hold for all of us.

I brought the memory stone with me, tucked into the inside pocket of my jacket. I could feel its warmth against my side. Several times that morning, I considered taking it out and pressing it to my forehead to see what would happen. If Jackson was telling the truth, I might gain some useful information, but if he wasn't, who knows what could happen. *If only there was someone who knew something about memory stones,* I thought as I carried on with my work. As soon as the realization hit me, I felt incredibly dumb. I had access to a mountain of useful information. One person I could always trust. Echo. "Zuki, I need to go," I called out.

She griped at me in a language I didn't understand, but I had to get away. "I'm sorry. I feel sick. I'll be back as soon as I can." I dropped the shovel and ran off with Zuki's disapproving voice ringing in my ears.

I raced through the circus grounds and found Echo strolling into the tent where he worked. The sun was finally coming up and the circus was bathed in a pink glow reflecting off the cloudy, red sky. "Echo, wait. Hey, can I ask you something?"

Echo started at my voice. "Sure," he said, reaching out to shake my hand. "What do you need?"

I glanced around to make sure we were alone. "Have you heard anything about today? Anything strange?"

Echo shook his head. "I don't know anything more than what I told you. If something is happening today, it isn't on record."

In that moment, I wondered if Jackson was wrong. Maybe Olivia was wrong too. I couldn't imagine an event so major happening without Echo knowing something about it. Maybe everyone was overreacting. "One more thing… have you ever heard of a memory stone?"

"Ooh, memory stones. Of course," Echo said. "They record memories. We have tons of them. Olivia keeps them locked away. Why do you ask?"

"So are they safe? Like, if I ever had the chance to use one? Is there any way things could go wrong?"

"They're perfectly safe. As safe as listening to a recording or watching a movie. Olivia and The Collector use them all the time."

"Thanks, Echo," I said. "Keep a look out for anything unusual."

"What do you mean? Is there something you aren't telling me? Do you know something?"

"I don't know anything for sure. I just want you to keep your eyes open."

"Will do," Echo said as he saluted, clicked his heels together, and marched away.

I was sprinting back toward the barns when Ember called out to me, chasing me up the path. "Hey, what are you doing?" she said. "Aren't you supposed to be working?"

"I am. I just had to ask Echo if he'd heard anything. And I wanted to see if he knew anything about memory stones."

"We're supposed to be going on with our day as normal, remember?" Ember said, barely above a whisper. "This is a big deal, Chase. We have to be careful."

"I know. I just thought, if it was safe, that it might be good to use the memory stone. There may find information we could use."

"Or it might melt your brain."

"I don't think so. I want to try it — see what's on it."

Ember's eyes grew big and her shoulders dropped. "Are you serious? You're really going to use that thing? You trust Jackson?"

"I don't know," I said. "I trust you and Echo; that's about it. But if The Collector is planning something that can hurt me, I need to know what it is. Or, at least, I need to know why."

Ember huffed. "Fine. But I'm going to be with you when you use it."

"Don't you have somewhere you're supposed to be?" I said. "Won't people notice if you're missing?"

"Look, we can talk about this all day, or we can just get it over with. If you're set on using that stone, then I'm going to be there. Period."

"Alright," I said. "Let's find somewhere quiet and see what this is all about. Maybe we can get back to our jobs before anyone realizes."

≈

A few minutes later, Ember and I were crouched behind an abandoned well on the edge of the grounds, staring down at the glowing, purple stone. I anxiously turned it over in my hand, examining it from all angles. I don't know what I hoped to see, but more than anything, I was trying to get the nerve to use it. "One last time...you're sure about this?" Ember said; the corner of her lip was upturned.

"I'm sure," I said, hoping to convince myself. "I need to know. Besides, I think it's safe. And if not...if it's some sort of trap, at least we'll know Jackson is a liar and that we can trust The Collector."

"Unless it kills you."

I nodded. "Unless it kills me."

Ember sat up straight and cleared her throat. "Alright, let's do it. I'm here if anything goes wrong. Get in, watch the memory, and get out."

"We can do this."

I lifted the warm, glowing stone toward my forehead. I could feel my mind reaching it, drawing me toward it, like

I was dying of thirst and the stone was a cool, clear river. "Wait," Ember said, grabbing my arm.

"What? What is it?"

"Nothing...I just...I..." Ember leaned over and kissed me. She pressed her lips to mine and a warm sensation filled my entire body before she slowly pulled away. "I just need you to know I care about you. That...I love you. I don't know what I'd do if something happens to you. And, just in case...I had to make sure you knew."

I placed my hand on Ember's arm and smiled. "It's going to be okay, Ember. I'll be back. Don't worry." And before I had time to doubt myself, I pressed the memory stone to my forehead.

The world around me swirled into blackness, and it felt like hundreds of tiny, warm tendrils were pulling free from the stone and attaching themselves to my mind. There was no pain or fear, just a dizzy sensation, similar to my sessions with Olivia. After a moment the darkness dissolved into a bright light. Sunlight. As soon as my eyes focused, I found myself standing in an open field of wildflowers on a cool spring morning. I was facing what seemed to be a small village in the valley below, with craggy, snow-peaked mountains that rose into a spotless blue sky. Fresh, clean air, and a gentle breeze made it all seem more like a fairytale than a memory. For a moment, I was lost in the quiet beauty of it. Then, I heard voices behind me. I turned to see a young man and woman sitting with legs crossed on a red and white checkered blanket. They laughed and chatted as they picked at a plate of fruit and cheese. Instantly, I knew the man was The Collector — a much younger version than the one I knew.

He still had the familiar confident presence and the same beaming smile, but there was something different about him. There was a certain playfulness I'd never noticed before. He seemed happy. Content.

The young woman, I'd never seen. She was pretty. Soft features and a shy smile. Her hair was pulled back and her gentle blond curls hung halfway down her back. I moved closer. Whatever Jackson wanted me to know, I figured it must have something to do with their discussion. I sat down next to them and listened in.

"You know, I still can't get over how fantastic your English is, Lynette," The Collector said.

"I told you, my mother and father insisted we learn English growing up," the young woman replied. She had a heavy French accent. "I just never knew it would come in so handy for talking to handsome young men." She dipped her head to the side and smiled again.

The Collector ran a hand through his hair before taking her hands in his own. "I don't want to be too forward, but there's something I think you should know."

"What is that?" Lynette said as she squeezed his hands.

"The last few days…being here with you. I've never felt so happy. I don't want to leave."

"Then don't, silly," she said, laughing. "Stay here with me." She motioned to the village below. "Look at this place. It's beautiful. We could be happy here."

"It is beautiful," The Collector said, staring at her hands. "That, I cannot deny. I have seen many beautiful sights on my travels, but I find none of them as fair as what I see before me now."

"Those are strong words, sir. I'm pleased you find my home so lovely."

"Oh, your home is lovely as well. But the beauty I find in this place, my dear, is because of you."

"You and your flattering words."

"My words are true. If you happen to find them flattering, then you know they only reflect my heart."

"Why, James?" she said, pleading. "Why do you have to go?"

"It's just...there...I have rules that I have to follow. It's complicated."

"Your work?"

"Yes," he said. "My work."

"When will you return?" Lynette asked.

The Collector lifted Lynette's hands to his face and softly kissed them. "I will return as soon as I possibly can. If all goes well, it will feel like no time has passed at all."

With those words, the sky blackened and the memory faded like ripples in a dark pool. A new memory began to take shape. I was inside someone's home. It was rustic and simple, but orderly and clean. An older woman was sweeping the knotted wooden floors and was humming an unfamiliar tune. She was interrupted by a knock on the door and propped her broom against the kitchen table. Muttering something in French, she pulled the door open and there, holding a bouquet of flowers, was the same young version of The Collector I'd seen earlier. "Mademoiselle," he said, taking a gentle bow. "May I speak to Lynette?"

"After all this time?" she said sharply.

"Yes, I'm sorry," The Collector said. "I returned as soon as I was allowed. Believe me, were it possible I'd of happily —"

"Mother?" Lynette said as she stepped out of her room. "Is everything okay?"

The Collector's face beamed with excitement. "Lynette?" he said as he pushed past her mother. He raced toward her. "Lynette, I'm so sorry it's taken me this long to get back to you. I never —"

"It's been over a year," Lynette answered coolly. "No letters. No word of when I might see you again. All I was left with were your empty promises."

"I understand," The Collector said. He placed the flowers on the kitchen table and wiped his hands against his blazer. "Please, if you'll allow me to explain…"

Lynette crossed her arms and turned her head. "I have little interest in hearing your explanations."

"Lynette…please."

The Collector and Lynette's mother stood there waiting for what felt like hours. Finally, Lynette whipped her head toward The Collector. "Fair warning…it better be a phenomenal explanation."

Again the scene shifted and turned, swirling into something altogether different. The Collector and Lynette were seated at a small iron table in front of her tiny home. Lynette was turned to the side, staring out toward the field beyond while The Collector was leaning in toward her, hands pressed against the table. "I know it's unfair to you that I've been away so long."

Lynette turned her steely gaze toward The Collector. "I waited for you." The Collector tried to continue, but Lynette spoke over him. "Everyday for the past year, I sat at home hoping you would send word. Praying that you were safe, that nothing horrible had happened to you. But there was nothing. I felt like such a fool."

The Collector took Lynette's hands, which she reluctantly allowed. "I wanted to come back to you, but I wasn't allowed."

"You weren't allowed?" she said. "Were you also prohibited from writing letters?"

"Yes," he said, pleading. "But I want to show you. I need you to understand that —" He paused and took a deep breath, his thoughts battling inside his mind. "Things aren't all that they seem. Some things are difficult to understand. Or to imagine even."

"James..." she began. "It's not that difficult. Not for me. The truth is, I don't trust you anymore, and I'm not sure if I ever can."

"Can I show you something?"

"It's not going to make a difference. I'm done listening to empty —"

"Let me show you. Then, if you want, I'll leave and you'll never have to see me again."

Lynette's gaze drifted away then back again. "Fine. Show me whatever you think will justify you disappearing for a year."

I had no more than blinked. When I opened my eyes, Lynette and The Collector were standing in the middle of the desert. Her hand was pressed tightly in his. "What is this?" she said. "Is this some sort of witchcraft?" She was gasping for air and was beginning to panic.

"It's alright, Lynette," The Collector said as he pulled her in close to him. "There's no witchcraft here. You're safe. I just had to prove it to you. I knew you wouldn't believe me if I simply told you."

Lynette's head was darting in all directions. "What did you do? Where are we?"

The Collector took her head in his hands and forced her eyes to him. "Lynette, listen to me," he said. "You are safe." She took a deep, settling breath, trying to calm herself. "I have an ability. I know it sounds odd, but just hear me. I can travel through space and time. There are many like me, each of us with abilities of our own."

"James, you sound insane."

"I know," he went on. "Trust me I know. I am from a time and place far from here. I was sent here, to your time, on a mission. We look for people. People with abilities like me."

"People who travel through time?"

"Some, yes. But there are people with all sorts of abilities. Some can move objects with their minds. Some can call lightning from the sky. The variations are limitless."

"Sorcery," Lynette whispered.

"It's not sorcery. It's ordinary people who can do fascinating things. These people, they are scattered all throughout time, and it's our job to check in on them. We make sure they're okay. We offer them the opportunity to join us."

Lynette shook her head as if she was attempting to shake off a cloud of fog. "So it's your job to find them? People with abilities? And you...you collect them?"

"I suppose you could call it that," he said with a laugh. "But most importantly, I make sure they're protected."

"This is difficult to hear, let alone understand."

"I know, but I had to tell you. See, I came here looking for others like me, but since I met you, I can't think of anything else. I stayed away so long because the people I work for wouldn't allow me to return. There are rules we must keep."

"Who are these people? Who do you work for?"

"We're called The Unseen. We are a community. A family. We protect one another and use our abilities to help others. I promise you...we are not witches, warlocks, or sorcerers. We're just people."

"Just people," she said. A sliver of a smile cracked her lips. "People who can do all sorts of strange things."

"Yes," he said with a relieved breath. "It's an incredible group."

"And you're their time traveler. The one who searches for others like them. The Collector."

"I like that," he said. "Perhaps I'll take that title for myself." He threw his arms open wide and called out in a loud voice. "All hail The Collector, the Master of Time and Space. Who, I might add, performs no witchcraft." Lynette laughed aloud and he went on. "And, by his side, the lovely, gentle, most beautiful woman to ever pass through time... the Magnificent, Lady Lynette." The Collector bowed with a great deal of fanfare as Lynette laughed and playfully cheered for him.

"Why here, James?" she said. "Of all the places in the world, why would you bring me to the middle of the desert?"

The Collector took her by the shoulders and slowly turned her around. "I wanted you to see something no one else can see." In the distance was the Great Pyramid of Giza.

Most of it anyway. It was in the process of construction. Though it wasn't in its final form, it was still an impressive sight to behold. A sturdy, stone tomb with a blazing, red sun settling into the horizon beyond.

Lynette gasped and lifted a hand to her mouth. "James, it's beautiful."

"An appropriate setting I think," he said. Right there in the sand, overlooking one of the wonders of the world, The Collector dropped to one knee and pulled out a ring. "Lynette, will you make me the happiest man to ever exist throughout all time? Will you marry me?"

"Of course," Lynette said as she threw herself into The Collector's arms. "But how? How will we be together? How does this work?"

The Collector flashed a handsome smile. "Come with me," he said. "Come back to The Unseen with me. If I bring you, they'll have to let you stay. We can work out all of the details then, but at least we'll be together."

Lynette pulled away a bit. "James, I — I can't just leave my family. My mother and father, they'd be heartbroken."

"You can tell them," he said pressing. "Tell them everything I told you. Tell them all about me and what I can do. I'll prove it to them if I need to. Don't you think they'll want you to be happy? There's no way they'd keep you from such an amazing opportunity."

"I just — I — I can't," she said. "Wh — Why don't you stay here? Stay with me. We could build a home and be happy. You could show me all the places I'd never get to see otherwise."

The Collector shook his head and dropped her hands.

"They'll never let me do that, Lynette. You have to under-stand, I'm bound to them. Lady Genevieve will never allow me to be with you. Not here. Not like this."

They both stood there in silence for a moment. There was only the sound of the wind whipping across the desert sands. Lynette stared down at the ring The Collector had placed on her finger, while he turned his back and stared into the sky. "I need time," Lynette said finally. "Time to prepare them. They won't understand."

The Collector spun around and raced back to her. "Yes, take as much time as you need."

"But, if I don't go with you now, when will I see you again? When will you be able to return?" Lynette asked, as a tear ran down her cheek.

"It will likely be another year," The Collector said. He wiped the tear away with his finger. "But please don't cry. If one year is what it costs to spend the rest of my life with you, it will have been worth it."

Lynette and The Collector embraced. The memory went black.

CHAPTER SEVENTEEN

My consciousness was still linked to the memory stone as another scene opened before me. I was back in the same small village, looking on as The Collector raced through the streets toward Lynette's house. He was adjusting his shirt and smoothing down his hair as he increased his pace. "Pardon," he said repeatedly as he bumped into various men and women who were strolling down the cobblestone streets. Under his left arm he carried a large powder blue box that he nearly dropped twice due to the pace he'd set. A broad smile was permanently fixed to his face, and he muttered to himself as he hurried along, rehearsing his upcoming conversation with Lynette. "Thank you for waiting. I've thought of you every day for the past year. I know it was difficult, but I promise I'll never leave your side again."

The Collector skipped up to the doorway of the small house and knocked boldly. After a moment, Lynette's mother opened the door. Her eyes were perfectly round and her mouth hung open. She looked at The Collector like someone would a mythical creature come to life. "You…" she said with a gasp.

He was unfazed. "Yes, it's me. And I'm here to see Lynette, please."

The woman shook her head slightly. "You...you nearly missed her."

The Collector's smile drooped and his brow furrowed. "Missed her? What do you mean? Is she leaving?" He pushed his way through the door. "Is she here?"

"Wait," her mother said, taking The Collector by the arm. "She's here, but...she's sick. Lynette...she won't be with us much longer."

The Collector pulled free from the woman's grasp and raced into Lynette's room. Lying there on her bed, under a mound of covers, was Lynette, a husk of the woman she had been a year earlier. Her skin was pale and her lips were slightly blue. With every labored breath, her chest rose and fell as she groaned in pain. Although it appeared she might be moments from death, still she smiled as The Collector entered the room. Lynette reached out a trembling hand and tried to speak, but no words would come out.

The Collector dropped the box he was holding. It collided with the ground and fell open; a white dress spilled out onto the dusty floor. "Lynette," he said with a gasp. "Lynette, what's wrong? What happened?"

"She has the fever," her mother said, stepping into the room behind him. "She's been this way for two months now. Suffering."

"What? How? I don't —" The Collector laid down across Lynette and began to weep. Tears flowed from his eyes and his body heaved with sorrow. He went on that way for a few agonizing minutes before gathering himself. He was making a plan. There was a spark of The Collector I knew. "Lynette, I will fix this. You're coming with me. I can get you help. I can take you away from here." Lynette was too weak to answer. The Collector turned to her mother. "I'm taking her now," he said. "As soon as I've found a doctor who can help her, I'll be back."

In an instant, we were standing in a hospital. The Collector was there. I was there. But Lynette was not. The Collector's arms were stretched out in front of him like he was carrying someone who didn't exist. The look on his tear stained face was one of shock and confusion. I blinked and we were back in Lynette's room. She was still lying on her bed. The Collector picked her up and held her tightly in his arms. Again, we were in the hospital. Lynette wasn't there. The Collector stared at his empty hands and began to frantically pace the waiting room. He grew more anguished with each step, eventually dropping to one knee and crying out in pain. Everyone turned their attention to him. "How could you?" he screamed as spit flew from his red face.

Once again, the memory faded to darkness.

As my thoughts began to refocus, I found myself in a dark room, lit with candles of all shapes, sizes, and colors. Flickering light danced on the walls, and the smell of smoke and incense was heavy in the air. The room was relatively empty with the exception of a large chair that sat against the far wall. It was made of bones with gold inlays and the skins of various animals. Two enormous white candles stood on either side of the chair like cathedral pillars. Their wax dripped down and puddled on the floor beneath them. In the chair was a large woman with dark, mottled skin. Her hair was in braids and dreads of several different colors that rose high above her head like a crown. She wore a deep red tunic of intricate design, and golden bracelets and dangled from her arms and fingers. She sat alone, staring forward, a grave expression on her face.

Suddenly, the door was thrown open and The Collector marched in. He had been crying and his usually flawless hair was a mess. The woman offered him no reaction as he stepped toward her; she simply nodded her head in greeting.

"How could you do this to me?" The Collector said, breathing heavily and shaking with anger.

"You did this to yourself, James," the woman said calmly. Her voice was rich and deep and even in such simple words, wisdom spilled from her.

"You know I love her. You know I can help her."

"This isn't something I can allow," she said. "It was made clear to you from the beginning."

"You allowed me to wait a year believing I would be with her. All the time, you knew it would never happen. You could have — you could have told me."

"I never had any intention of telling you what to do. I'm not some general that gives orders. Given time, I hoped you'd see reason. You know there are rules governing this sort of —"

"And who makes those rules?" he screamed, jabbing a finger toward her. "You? The powerful Lady Genevieve, sitting on her throne bestowing wisdom on all of us lowly peasants?"

"Do not storm in here and speak to me like a child," Lady Genevieve said with a slight edge to her voice. "I don't create the rules anymore than you do. The council, of which I am a part, creates the rules. No one forced you into this society. You chose to join us. You chose to abide by our laws."

"Fine then," The Collector said. "I want out."

"So, that's it? You want out? You want to be on your own?"

"Yes," he said bluntly. "I choose not to be a part of this cult-like gathering of freaks. Remove my mark."

Lady Genevieve paused and studied him for a moment. "Are you certain this is what you want?"

The Collector stood up as straight as he could. "I am. I've never been more certain of anything."

"You do realize this won't change what has happened. And it certainly won't make you free of the rules that govern people such as we are."

"I refuse to spend another moment serving under someone as heartless and ruthless as you. Now, remove the mark."

"Jackson…" Lady Genevieve said. Her eyes were still on The Collector. From the shadows Jackson appeared, wearing his white shirt and green bow tie.

"Yes, Lady Genevieve?" he said.

"Remove the mark from James."

Jackson stepped up behind The Collector and placed his hand over the mark. The Collector was unflinching as Jackson's hand began to glow and the mark was drawn from his skin. When he finished, Jackson stepped away and retreated into the shadows.

"I *will* find a way around this," The Collector said. "I will be with Lynette. You will not stop me."

Lady Genevieve sat up in her chair. "As much as you

may not believe this or want to hear it…I love you, James. I never wanted to hurt you."

The Collector huffed and wiped a tear from his face. "Yeah, well…you won't ever hurt me again."

"I wish you well, James."

The Collector gave her one last look. A look filled with such intense rage, I thought he might attack her at any moment. Instead, he turned sharply and walked away. Lady Genevieve sat there in the soft light of the flickering candles for a moment before turning her gaze to me. She stared at me as if it weren't a memory at all. As if she knew I had been there all along. I stood still as I could, unsure if I should speak or not. Then, Lady Genevieve spoke. "You are his key," she said. The darkness swallowed the candlelight and the memory was gone.

There was a sound like howling wind as the tendrils of the memory stone release their grip on my mind. I squinted into the bright sunlight and gave my eyes a moment to adjust. The weight of everything I'd just witnessed was too heavy for me to keep to myself. But when I turned to tell Ember what I'd learned, I found myself alone. It was a all so eerily quiet. "Ember?" I called out. There was no answer. I jumped to my feet and shielded my eyes while I scanned my surroundings. It wasn't like Ember to leave me in such a vulnerable position. Something was wrong. I took a deep breath to call out for her again when a searing pain shot through the mark on the back of my neck. It was a pain like I'd never experienced before, like a jolt of electricity. From across the grounds, I heard a collective howl of pain from what I assumed was everyone with a mark like mine. The other members of the circus. Without wasting another moment, I raced toward the distant sounds of pain. My best guess was that everyone was gathered in one place. The center of the circus. The Cauldron of Kinship. My thoughts were reeling with all of the terrible things that might be happening. Were my friends safe? Was the circus in danger? Was The Collector finally carrying out his plan?

As I drew nearer, I realized my hunch was right. There, gathered around the cauldron, was every member of the circus. All of The Lost. And in the middle of the crowd stood The Collector, dressed in his best clothes as if he were ready to open the gates and let the public in. He saw me while I was still approaching. His eyes caught mine, and the look on his face was without emotion. It was as if the spirit of the man had left him and all that was left was the cold outer shell. He was empty but determined.

"Silence," The Collector called out as he held up his hands. The voices hushed as I pressed through the crowd. "I apologize for calling you all here so abruptly, but there is an urgent matter at hand. One to which you must bear witness." I made my way to the front of the onlookers and stood facing The Collector. He didn't seem to notice me as he continued with his speech. "As you are certainly aware, loyalty to this family is a trait I require of everyone who calls this home. If this circus is to be a safe haven for those with abilities, it is imperative that a mutual trust exists." I forced myself to stop grinding my teeth and unclench my jaw. The warning from Jackson was ringing in my ears as I scanned the crowd looking for Ember and Echo. There was no sign of them.

Luka and Analise parted the crowd and suddenly appeared next to The Collector. "Sir," Analise said with a dip of her head.

"Are we ready?" The Collector asked. She nodded. He turned his focus back to the circus members and announced aloud, "Please make your way to the main tent. I have something prepared for you."

Everyone immediately began to disperse, mumbling as they went. I stayed behind, hoping to have a word with The Collector. "Is everything okay?" I said.

The Collector looked at me with blank eyes. "Make your way to the tent, Chase."

"Are Ember and Echo okay? They aren't here and —"

"Make your way to the tent," he said slowly through gritted teeth. "Now, please."

I didn't press my luck. I turned and followed the crowd, leaving The Collector, Luka, and Analise behind. Once inside, I was struck by how silent it was. Everyone found a seat quickly and waited for whatever was about to happen. I felt sick to my stomach as I continued looking for my friends. Suddenly, the lights went out and a spotlight found The Collector who stood center stage.

"Good day, my friends," he said. "I stand before you today a hurting man. Damaged by the bitter taste of betrayal." He dropped his gaze and continued. "There are some among us who have kept secrets, told lies, and basically undermined the integrity of our family. For such sins, there must be retribution."

Two more spotlights cut through the dark room, illuminating their marks on either side of The Collector. My heart sank and my throat tightened. There, in font of a gasping crowd, were Ember and Echo, both bound to the floor with heavy chains connected to iron shackles clasped around their wrists and ankles. Ember stood still with a hateful scowl on her face while Echo twisted and wiggled, wrestling against his restraints. Without thinking, I leaped to my feet, determined to help my friends. But at that same moment, a crippling pain clamped down on my neck and my knees buckled. I fell face-first onto the floor by my seat. Analise's mark had rendered me immobile. Those closest to me quickly reached down and lifted me back into my seat. I was too stunned and in too much pain to move.

The Collector continued his show; his voice boomed throughout the tent. "First, allow me bring to your attention the crimes committed by my once trusted Seer you know as Echo." Echo immediately ceased his struggling and glared wide-eyed at The Collector. Beads of sweat dripped down his face. "You see, dear friends, Echo's rather unique skills make him invaluable to this circus as it pertains to locating and recruiting new members. However, those same skills give him access to extremely sensitive information. Information he made a vow to keep secret. That vow included never endangering this circus or its members by sharing anything he learned. Well, not only did he share knowledge he gained through deceptive means, he also put all of our lives at risk by doing so." There was a collective gasp from the crowd. Echo began to cry. "Today, he will pay for his transgressions."

The boy sitting next to me leaned over and asked, "Did he really do that?"

I wanted to tell him "no," but my throat was still clinched and my neck was burning from whatever hold Analise had on me. And if I was being honest, there was some truth to The Collector's words.

The Collector turned his attention away from Echo to Ember. She didn't look scared at all. She looked angry. With fiery eyes, she glared hatefully at The Collector. "As egregious as his actions may be, the misdoings of Echo are only surpassed by those of our star, Ember." Those seated around me sat up straight and stretched out their necks to see what would happen next. To hear what The Collector would say. "Ember not only left the circus grounds without permission, she had an altercation with a local and used her abilities in his presence." Again, those present reacted with quick hushed comments to one another. "She was also privy to the information Echo shared and was aware an outsider had infiltrated our circus." The Collector raised his voice above the murmuring crowd. "Not only was she aware of this intruder, she also spoke to him." He jabbed his finger toward her. "This girl discovered that he stood in opposition to the ideals by which we live. To the family we have created. That he intended to *rescue* some of you from my apparently tyrannical reign." The crowd sat in stunned silence as The Collector lowered his voice. "And perhaps, worst of all…she said nothing. She gave me no warning. Not one single act she took served to protect the men and women of this family."

It was painfully quiet. Those sitting nearby shot nervous glances in my direction. I couldn't blame them. I was nervous myself. For one, I should have been sitting on that stage right alongside of Ember and Echo. I was just as guilty as they were. The fact that I wasn't was even more terrifying. I had no idea what The Collector had in mind, but if what Jackson said was correct, my role in this display would be coming soon. My decision was already made. If I had to choose between letting Echo and Ember be harmed or The Collector harming me, then my choice would be to keep them safe. I knew they would do the same for me.

"As much as it pains me to do so," The Collector went on, "I have no other alternative. Please know that this is done out of love for you all. My foremost duty is to protect you. Therefore, the punishment for such offenses is simple. Echo and Ember must be Forsaken."

CHAPTER EIGHTEEN

IT HAPPENED SO quickly, there was no time to react. As fast as snapping your fingers, Ember and Echo were gone. Everyone gathered in the main tent that day stood up and frantic chatter broke out among the group like a wave of fear. I tried to stand as well, but the mark on my neck stabbed at me again and I fell back into my seat. I glanced over to see Analise patrolling the aisle with a watchful eye on me. My body was numb and my heart ached. My two closest friends in the world had just become Forsaken. Lost in time. Sent away to some time and place where I'd never be able to find them.

"Please, take your seats," The Collector announced. "I realize this may come as a shock for you. Ember and Echo were valuable members of our family, but, in the end, they were disloyal to both you and me. Please, sit down now. There is yet another matter that requires action." The muffled talk continued as the circus members slowly took their seats.

This is it, I thought. Whatever The Collector had planned for me, it was about to happen. My first thought is that I would become Forsaken myself. But if that was the case, I probably would have been sent away with Ember and Echo. If The Collector planned on using my friends as leverage to draw out my ability, then banishing them was a mistake. I was shaken, but I was also angry. Whatever he wanted from me, he wouldn't get it. My hope was that Jackson would show up with the rest of The Unseen to rescue me. I'd stall as long it took. The Collector would not have the satisfaction of discovering my ability. I'd take any punishment he dished out, but his only hold on me had just been sent away. Or so I thought.

Luka stepped out from backstage, pushing a large domed structure. It was draped with a pale blue, satin covering and its wheels squeaked as he found his mark, center stage. "Thank you, Luka," The Collector said. "Ladies and gentlemen, this is the last bit of business we'll need to attend to today. Admittedly, action of this nature should not occur within these gates, and I promise you I'd avoid it if I had any other option. Analise, bring him up."

The mark on my neck buzzed and I jumped to my feet. Analise was standing at the end of the aisle and simply pointed me toward the stage. I could hear the murmuring around me. Whispering voices carrying on conversations about me. Wondering what had happened. What I had done. What would happen. My first instinct was to run, but I knew it wouldn't help. There was nowhere to run and no one to run to. With stone-like determination, I stepped up onto the stage where my friends had just been. A stage where now there was only The Collector, Luka, and me. And whatever was under that covering.

The Collector placed his hand on my shoulder. I shirked away, but I didn't want to make too much of a scene. There was no need to give him further reason to justify whatever he was about to do. He addressed the circus. "For those of you who may not be aware, this is Chase. He has been with us for two years now; a lost soul in need of the sort of support and care this environment provides. I found him, took him in, made him part of our family, and did the best I could to ensure his safety and nurture his manifestation. If you know Chase, then you also know that Ember and Echo were his close friends." He removed his hand from my shoulder. "And when it comes to jeopardizing the safety of this circus and its members, he is no less guilty than they."

I wanted to yell at him. To shout his sad story out to everyone. Try hurt him as much as he had hurt me. Instead, I fumed in silence. It was like burning coals were scorching my insides and I didn't know how long I'd be able to hold my anger. The Collector continued. "However, I am a patient man. I am willing to offer Chase an opportunity to correct his wrongdoing." The crowd chattered as The Collector left my side and stepped up in front of the covered structure. "I know you all may be asking yourselves, 'Why would he forgive Chase for these most heinous actions?' Well, the truth is, Chase has an ability that could benefit all of us. A power that could atone for his actions several times over. Forsaking Chase may be less beneficial to this family than allowing him to remain and providing him the opportunity for restoration. Chase is special and his ability is rare. Olivia and I believe that Chase is a Healer."

My jaw dropped, and my mind shut down nearly all sound and movement in the room. I was stunned. Plunged into some sort of dreamlike state. It was the first time I'd been given any clue as to what my ability might be. I scanned the room and caught Olivia's eye. She was looking straight at me and mouthed the words, "I'm sorry." I barely had time to process any of it before The Collector spoke over the crowd and continued with his presentation. "However, because of his transgressions, I find it necessary to take immediate, albeit drastic, action. Analise, if you will."

Analise stepped up and pulled the satin covering from the structure. Underneath was a black, wrought iron cage with a domed top, like a giant birdcage. Inside, crouching in the center, was a terribly frightened girl. A girl with long brown hair and a tear stained face. I knew immediately who it was. Sophia. "Chase?" she said with a shaky voice. "Chase, what's happening?"

Before I could answer, The Collector turned to Sophia and spoke loud enough for the entire tent to hear. "Hello, young lady," he said. "Allow me to apologize for putting you in such an uncomfortable situation." Sophia flinched at his words and at that moment realized not only was she held captive, but she was on display. Like a cornered rabbit, her eyes darted in all directions, looking for any means of escape. If she was the rabbit, The Collector was the wolf. There was no escape. "If all goes according to plan, Sophia, you'll have nothing to worry about." He turned back to the circus members. "I will ask Luka to inflict this young girl with a life-threatening illness. One that will course through her veins like deadly poison. Without intervention, she will pass within minutes. However, if our assessment is correct, Chase will manifest and heal her, saving her from a most gruesome and painful death."

"Chase, what's happening?" Sophia called out in a panicked voice.

"I'm sorry," I said. "I didn't know anything about this."

"And I am sorry as well," The Collector said to her. "I am sorry that Chase's actions have placed you in such a predicament." He paused. "Now, Luka, if you will."

Luka stepped forward and reached through the bars of the cage for Sophia. She pressed herself against the far side. "Get away from me," she screamed. The circus members rose to their feet, straining to get a better look. Luka was undeterred. He moved to the gate, opened it, and stepped inside. Sophia rushed him, punching and kicking, but Luka was much too powerful. He grabbed her wrists, and as soon as his bare hands touched her skin, a look of terror and pain washed over her face. Sophia immediately went pale. Her lips turned white, her eyes rolled back, and she collapsed. Luka stepped out of the cage and shot an emotionless glance at me before returning to his post.

My eyes went to The Collector and my voice cracked. "Why? Why would you do this?"

For an instant, I was sure I saw a look of remorse in his eyes. I could have sworn he was about to call it all off. That he would end the spectacle, have Luka reverse whatever he'd done, and send Sophia home. However, his brief moment of empathy passed as quickly as I'd noticed it and The Collector's face hardened. "Go to her, Chase. Save her if you can."

With the entire circus looking on, I ran to Sophia, threw open the cage door, and dropped to my knees beside her. "Sophia, Sophia," I said as I pulled her head up onto my lap.

She was ghostly white and I thought she might already be dead. "Sophia, can you hear me?"

She stirred a bit. Moaned and barely opened her eyes. "Chase," she managed to choke through her groans.

I knew I was supposed to heal her. The pressure of the situation was intended to make me manifest. I was supposed to save her. But I had no idea how how to do it. I felt nothing. There was no stirring of power inside of me, no feeling of strength. There was only dreadful panic. "Sophia," I whispered in her ear. "Sophia, I'm sorry."

I pressed my face to hers, and felt her eyelashes flutter against my cheek. I pulled away and saw her staring at me with milky, dull eyes. It was as if she was looking right through me. Seeing something I couldn't see. Her voice was thin and frail. "Chase, I…Something's wrong…I…"

A hand clamped down on my shoulder. "I suppose this experiment has failed," The Collector said quietly. At that moment, there was a deep rumbling like an thunder rolling under our feet. The floor shook and rocked and the large wooden beams that held the tent in place began to rock and crack. The circus members cried out in panic and raced toward the exit. "Analise," The Collector called out. "What is this?"

"I don't know," she answered. "I can't stop it. I don't think it's one of us."

"Well, find out," he screamed.

The words had no sooner left his mouth when a great gust of wind tore through the grounds and ripped the canvas top completely free of the main tent. The sky above was blood red with dingy gray clouds swirling like ghosts above us.

Lightning streaked across the horizon and struck the ground both inside and outside of the tent, leaving black craters and the smell of burnt earth and smoke. The skeletal like frame of the tent began to shudder and bend as if the entire structure might give way at any moment. The Collector pulled me away from Sophia and handed me off to Luka. "Get him out of here," he cried. "Take him somewhere safe."

I fought against Luka, but his grip was strong and no matter how much I kicked and squirmed, he wouldn't let go. Debris flew everywhere and between the lightning strikes and strong winds, Luka inched slowly toward the exit. I glanced over his shoulder, back at Sophia. She was trying to sit up. Trying to escape. But she was weak and frail, like an old lady whose legs no longer supported her. Next to her stood The Collector, Olivia, and Analise. Given the extreme storm blowing through, they should have been running for cover. Instead The Collector was pointing and waving his arms around, screaming something about how he couldn't believe they let something like this happen. It was difficult to hear, but Olivia and Analise were definitely catching the blame for whatever had caused the unnatural storm. I watched as Sophia collapsed onto the floor of the cage, and I shut my eyes tight as Luka carried me out of the tent like a laundry bag. Outside, trees were cracking in two, rain was falling like stinging needles, and lightning continued to strike at will. Sirens wailed in the distance and circus members scrambled for any shelter they could find.

Another deep rumble came up from the earth and Luka nearly fell as the ground rocked like waves beneath his feet. It was followed by a loud boom, like a cannon blast, and instantly, everything went silent. The storm had ended as suddenly as it had begun. Luka stopped in his tracks and I opened my eyes to a perfectly normal, sunny day. The winds were calm. The sky was a peaceful shade of blue, and birds chirped in the distance. That day was also the first time I'd ever heard Luka speak. "Did you do this?" he said. "Did you cause the storm? Or stop it?" He put me down, but kept his hand clasped tightly around my wrist.

"It wasn't me. I didn't do it. At least I don't think I did."

He began to speak but was interrupted by a woman's voice. "Let the boy go, Luka," she said. We both turned to see Lady Genevieve, Jackson, and a woman I didn't recognize. She had long dark hair, wild and untamed, and wore a bright red overcoat. Whereas Lady Genevieve moved slowly and deliberately, the woman with her stepped heavily and scanned her surroundings as if she was looking for a fight.

Luka grabbed me and pulled me in close, his arm clamped around my neck. "Stay away," he said. "I don't want to hurt him."

"Come now, we both know that won't happen," Lady Genevieve said as she stepped toward us. Luka stared silently for a moment. His breathing picked up and I could feel the tension in his body as he gripped me tightly. "Just move aside."

With speed I couldn't have imagined Luka capable of, he threw me aside and lunged at Lady Genevieve. She didn't flinch. She didn't have to. The lady in the bright red coat threw her hands out in front of her and Luka ran headlong into an invisible barrier. Like a translucent wave, the barrier rippled and with a loud thud, Luka fell to the ground, unconscious.

Lady Genevieve looked down at me and smiled. "Hello, Chase," she said, extending her hand. "I need you to come with us." Slowly, I placed my hand in hers as Lady Genevieve pulled me to my feet.

The woman in red spoke. "We have company."

"How dare you trespass on this ground," The Collector called as he and Analise raced toward us. "You have no right to be here."

Lady Genevieve seemed undeterred. "Do you honestly intend to lecture me on my rights, James?"

"I'd advise you not to call me by that name," The Collector said through gritted teeth. "That man was lost long ago. You of all people should know that."

"I'm not here to debate you," Lady Genevieve said. "I'm only here for the boy."

The Collector smiled. "Then I'm afraid we find ourselves in a grim predicament. I have no intention of losing him to you."

Lady Genevieve spread her arms wide. "Come now, there's no need in digressing to the point of winners and losers. Certainly we can come to an agreement. Tell me, what do you suggest?"

"Analise," The Collector said, his eyes still on Lady Genevieve. "How taxing would it be for you to suppress all three of these intruders while we decide on a suitable punishment for their trespassing?"

Analise retained her typical stoic expression. "It would be my pleasure," she said.

"To what end? You have your Suppressor, I have mine," Lady Genevieve said, motioning to Jackson. "We'd do little more than reduce this to a heated argument that could ramble on indefinitely."

"Then once again, you woefully underestimate me." The Collector paused to flash his well-rehearsed smile before calling out in a loud voice: "Men and women of this great circus, there are intruders among us. They wish nothing more than to hurt and destroy the society we've worked so diligently to build. Protect this circus. Protect this family. Unite and show them we stand as one."

With a great shout like a war cry, the members of the circus came flooding onto the midway, surrounding us. Some held makeshift weapons, sticks, or rocks. Others stood at the ready, waiting to use their abilities if needed to defend themselves. On their faces was a mixture of hate and fear. I had known those people for years, but never before had I seen them like that. Scared and angry, standing there breathing heavily and waiting for The Collector to give the word to attack. They weren't soldiers, and they certainly weren't killers. They were a panic-stricken group of men and women, boys and girls, all ready to fight for The Collector's cause. There was a time I would have stood with them, red-faced with my heart thumping in my chest. That was before Jackson gave me the memory stone. Before I knew The Collector's story. Before Ember and Echo were Forsaken.

CHAPTER NINETEEN

Most people would wither being surrounded by such an angry, powerful mob, but Lady Genevieve hardly seemed to notice. Her eyes were fixed on The Collector. "This is a terrible idea, James. Surely you know there's no favorable ending here. Not for you. Not for them. Not for any of us."

"Then what do you suggest, madam?" he said through a smug grin.

"We're taking the boy," she replied firmly. "You will stand aside and let us do what we came here to do. We'll take him and go peacefully."

He motioned to me. "Perhaps *the boy* doesn't want to go with you. But I suppose that detail wouldn't deter you, would it?"

"So now you point fingers at me? Accuse me of forcing others into my bidding after I watch you execute a poor girl in front of your followers? Even someone as blinded by hate as you can see the irony."

The Collector's smile melted away, and when he spoke, the words dripped like poison from his lips. "As distasteful as my actions may be to you, at least I act out of love. You discard those who might be saved out of some misguided sense of loyalty to antiquated ideals. Ideals handed down to us by those who lack in power but excel in control. You allow people to die when you have the power to save them, and you lecture me about abusing power? What gives you the right to decide how I apply my God-given gift?"

"The council gives me the right."

"I *reject* the council," The Collector screamed. The rest of us looked on in silence. "The council has done nothing for me, but attempt to dictate my actions and keep me from the one thing I love in this world. You speak of justice and transparency but you rule out of jealousy and fear."

"You and I have walked this road many times over," she said. "As much as the fact pains me, I'm afraid there's nothing left for us to discuss."

"That's not a decision you get to make. Not any more. Not for me."

"So you have something more to say? A logical reason that would convince me to go and leave Chase here with you?"

The Collector looked my way. His eyes opened wide and fresh realization washed over him. "I see what's happening here. I was right, wasn't I?" he said to Lady Genevieve. "I was right about Chase being a Healer. You've kept him from me, haven't you? You took away his choice. You've hidden him from his destiny."

"I saved you from yourself," Lady Genevieve said. "Or at least I'm trying to."

"It all makes sense now. You've had your hands in this from the beginning. You knew he was a Healer, so you prevented him from manifesting." He jabbed an angry finger back toward the tent. "The truth is, you allowed the girl he cared for to die simply out of spite. You'd do anything to keep control over me, and you used Chase to do it. He doesn't know, does he? Chase doesn't know you've been suppressing his ability."

Genevieve frowned and deep, dark creases formed along her forehead. "You are truly delusional if you believe I'd allow that girl to suffer in order to spite you." Genevieve paused. "Besides, Chase knows more than you may think."

"Is that so? Please tell me what lies you've filled his head with."

Genevieve cast an ominous look my way, then back to The Collector. "He's seen the memory stone. Chase is aware of what's happened."

The Collector snarled a bit. "I'm sure he was made privy to the pieces you chose. The memories you needed him to see. Those that portray you as the champion of justice while I come across as some sort of crazed criminal." His eyes cut to me.

"And which details of Chase's life have you kept hidden from him?" she said. The Collector's face turned blood red but he didn't respond. Lady Genevieve let the silence sit for a moment. "He saw what happened. Nothing more."

"What *happened?* My life is not some event that came and went and is over and done. It's still happening. You are forcing this grief and pain upon me. You interjected yourself into my life and made me an enemy when all I ever did was blindly serve you."

There was a noticeable sadness on Lady Genevieve's face. A look that suggested her heart ached as much as The

Collector's. "I understand how you feel. You've made yourself entirely clear. However, we have a more pressing issue. Where do you suggest we go from here?" Lady Genevieve glanced at the crowd that pressed in on us. "You have Analise. I have Jackson. With a word, everyone here would be suppressed and we'd find ourselves at a stalemate."

"Not quite," The Collector said. "You forget where you are. This is our home. We have numbers. Suppressing these men and women may hinder their abilities, but it won't stop them from tearing you to shreds."

Lady Genevieve dropped her head and nodded. "You do appear to have the advantage, and you could do just as you said. But you are also wise enough to know the council would not look favorably on such action. You would be hunted down. Your abilities would be stripped."

The Collector's face went rigid, like a man who'd just determined to burn the world down around him. I knew he'd never back down. He wouldn't surrender me without a fight. When he spoke, his words were icy and calloused. "Let the council come for me," he said. "They'll meet the same fate as you." He briefly glanced around before announcing, "Citizens of this great circus, these are our enemies. Finish them."

The mob rushed in as both Analise and Jackson raised their hands, but the back of my neck barely had time to prickle before all was still. It was the same feeling I had when The Collector had paused time and saved me from Julius' drunken knife throwing. The air was thick and heavy and everyone looked like they'd been dropped into a cauldron of molasses. Stuck in place. Everyone that is except for The

Collector and Lady Genevieve. "You can't hold them forever," The Collector said. Eventually you'll tire, and —"

"And what, James?" Lady Genevieve said. "Then you'll let them kill me?"

"Oh, don't be so dramatic," he said. "I'll treat you the same way any law-abiding civilization would treat trespassers and those who wish to do harm. I'll capture you, lock you away, schedule a trial, and let the people decide."

"So that makes you the leader of this country? The wise king, keeping watch over his kingdom?"

"Yes, I am their leader. I am their leader because they choose me. They believe in what we've built here. What we stand for."

"What you've built is an illusion. You play the caring leader while you use the power it affords to serve your own ends."

The Collector nodded. "I do benefit from the faith they place in me. We benefit from one another. We are a family. They need me just as much as I need them. Someone has to look out for those who've been depleted and abused by such treacherous authority. Everyone deserves the right to be free."

"Free? Like those you've freed lately? What are they called? Forsaken?"

"You know nothing about our ways," The Collector said with a snarl. "Anyone Forsaken, is so because they deserve to be."

"I have found some who disagree," Lady Genevieve said. No sooner had she spoken than there was a slight ripple and a thump nearby. The three of us turned to see someone I thought I'd never see again. Setu.

"I am here, Lady Genevieve," my old friend Setu said in his deep voice. My heart leaped with joy, but I tried to keep quiet. Setu glanced down at me and smiled. "Are you ready for me to take the boy now?"

"Setu, you're back," The Collector said. "And I see you've joined my enemy. Learned some new tricks?"

Setu turned his eyes to The Collector. "New tricks?"

The Collector raised his arms and glanced around the grounds. "The storm, the lightning, the dark, foreboding sky. It was very impressive."

Lady Genevieve spoke, "We thought the illusion came from within the circus. It wasn't us."

All eyes turned to me. I didn't think I had done anything like that, but at that point, I was completely confused. For all I knew, it very well had been me.

"Shall I take him?" Setu said. His tone made it clear he was becoming uncomfortable.

"Traitor," The Collector said. "I was right to send you away."

Setu motioned for me to come closer, so I stepped over next to him. He placed his arm around me and spoke to The Collector. "I served you faithfully for years. Never once did I dream of betraying you. You are not the man you once were. You take us and use us and mask it all with a smile that fools us into believing you do it for our own good."

The Collector dropped his arms and his shoulders sagged. "That hurts, Setu," he said, seemingly sincere.

"Not as much as it has hurt me," Setu replied.

"Lady Genevieve, don't do this," The Collector said. It was the first time that day I'd noticed anything other than anger or sarcasm in his voice. I thought he might try to reason with her, but I soon learned different. "I know you must be growing weary of holding all of these people suspended in time. If you allow Setu to take Chase, I'll be forced to pull them from your hold. I think we both know what happens then."

Lady Genevieve didn't flinch. Her resolve held firm. "You are somewhat correct. I won't be able to hold them much longer. However, we will be taking Chase and I will be joining them."

"You are forcing my hand," The Collector said.

"No, you are forcing mine. I can't hold them much longer, but I do have enough strength to send them all away. I'll deal with them the same way you handle the Forsaken. I'll scatter them to the winds of time. I'll hide them so well, it will take you the rest of your life to track them down. And I know how valuable your time is."

"You wouldn't dare," he said. "Even you aren't that cruel."

"I'll do what I must to survive. And to ensure Chase is safe."

The Collector smiled. "So you and I are the same."

"We're probably more alike than you know," Lady Genevieve replied. "Which is why you know what you have to do."

"Very well," The Collector said. He straightened his collar and buttoned his coat as if he was about to take the stage. "This round goes to you. But as certain as the stars in the sky, we will meet again, Lady Genevieve." Then he looked at me. "I've enjoyed our last two years together, Chase. I have a feeling our story won't end here today. When you discover, as many have, that Lady Genevieve isn't as honorable as she appears, you'll want out. And I'll be waiting for you."

Within the span of a blink, The Collector, his followers, and every canvas, frame, and rope that made up the circus were gone. Standing alone in the empty lot were Setu, Lady Genevieve, and me. Apparently, Lady Genevieve had been struggling more than she'd allowed The Collector to know. As soon as he'd left and taken the circus with him, Lady Genevieve dropped to her knees, utterly exhausted. Setu rushed from my side to help her. "Are you alright?" he said. "Just relax, I'll get us all back." Then to me he said, "Come over here, Chase. Join hands and I'll take us somewhere safe."

I took a couple of steps toward Setu when a faint sound grabbed my attention, something like a whimper. I spun around and saw Sophia in the distance. She was attempting to crawl toward us. She was incredibly weak, but still alive. "Chase, help me," Sophia said, although her voice was barely audible.

"Setu, we have to help her."

"There's nothing we can do for her, Chase. Luka has ensured that. We must leave now. We have to get Lady Genevieve to safety."

"No," Lady Genevieve said with a groan. "Let him go to her. He can help."

I took off running toward Sophia before Setu had any chance to protest. Lady Genevieve said I was a Healer. She admitted to suppressing my ability to manifest. So I didn't know how to use my ability, but if Lady Genevieve said I could help Sophia, I had to try. By the time I reached her, Sophia was unconscious again. Her skin was unnaturally white and she was foaming slightly from the corner of her mouth. I dropped to my knees and placed her head in my lap. Her skin was far too cold and whatever life remained in her was fading quickly. If I had known how to heal her, I certainly would have, but I had no idea what I was supposed to do. I sat there in a numb panic, gently pulling strands of hair from her sweaty forehead and attempting to swallow the thick lump forming in my throat. "I'm sorry," I whispered in her ear.

It was the first time I felt the power rising inside of me. My heart began to race and my hands grew warm. With nothing to guide me but my instincts, I hurriedly pushed up her sleeves and took hold of her forearms. I didn't know why, but I was certain my hands needed to touch her skin.

Something happened.

Not only was the heat intensifying, but I noticed my hands began to glow. It was barely noticeable at first, but as I held onto Sophia's arms, my hands grew brighter and warmer until they were as bright as the headlights on a car. I stared down at the warm golden light enveloping my hands, amazed at what I saw. That's when I felt it for the first time. It's difficult to describe, but it felt like my hands were literally drawing the sickness out of Sophia's body. It hurt. A dull, aching pain like an intense headache, except the sensation traveled throughout my entire body. Sophia's eyes began to flutter behind her closed lids, and it was only a moment later when the color rushed back to her face and she started to groan.

"Keep going," Lady Genevieve said into my ear as she placed a hand on my shoulder. I started at her words, but it did help me feel like my instincts had been correct. Whatever Luka had done to her, whatever sickness he'd inflicted upon Sophia — I was taking it away. Drawing it out of her like thin strands of disease, one by one. Although I didn't know how it worked, I could tell it was effective.

After a few moments more, Sophia's eyes sprang open and she took in a huge gasp of air. She bolted upright and grabbed hold of me, pulling me in close to her. "Thank you, Chase," she said with a weak voice. "I don't know what you did, but thank you. Thank you for saving me."

It would have been embarrassing to admit, but part of me enjoyed that moment. Sitting there with Sophia's arms around me, thanking me for saving her. Being proud of myself for finally manifesting. It was a great moment. Great until the nausea hit. It came on fast and slammed into me like a speeding truck. I tore myself away from Sophia and ran. I only made it a couple of steps before I threw up. It sounds disgusting but it wasn't a normal sick. It was like a full body heave meant to purge my insides of whatever that disgusting black bile was that flooded out. My head swam and my sight grew fuzzy around the edges. I turned to look at Sophia, Lady Genevieve, Jackson, and the woman in the red coat. They all seemed concerned, but perhaps not surprised. Jackson took a step toward me. I took once last look at Sophia before I passed out.

CHAPTER TWENTY

I WOKE UP in a dark room with only a few flickering candles to help make out my surroundings. It was warm, and the bed I was lying in was soft with plenty of blankets. Fabrics of all different colors and designs lined the windowless walls and the smell of sweet incense filled the air. Beside the bed was a simple wooden table where a clump of half-melted candles sat, red and white wax pooling and dripping onto the splintered floor. I sat up slowly on the edge of the bed, a bit dizzy and disoriented. Just as my bare feet touched the wooden floor, the door opened and Jackson entered. "Chase, you're awake," he said cheerfully. He was carrying a tray with a glass of orange juice and a single piece of buttered toast. "I'm glad I decided to move forward with the toast."

"How long have I been out?" I asked, rubbing my head.

Jackson paused to think. "Nearly an entire day. Twenty two hours to be exact. Your friends have been worried sick about you, but Lady Genevieve assured them you'd be fine. Once again, she was right. She usually is."

"My friends?"

"Oh, I nearly forgot," Jackson said as he set the tray on the bed next to me. "No one's had a chance to tell you.

We've been monitoring The Collector very closely over the last few months. We've managed to track every person he had Forsaken. Through a little hard work and an excellent Seer, we were able to locate almost everyone, so…we went and got them."

"You mean, Ember and Echo?"

"Yes, they are here and doing well. You should get to see them soon."

I took a deep breath and felt the tensions leave my shoulders. Knowing Ember and Echo were safe was better for my recovery than the entire day of sleeping. My eyes scanned the room again. "Where exactly are we?"

"*Where* and *when*, you mean," he said, lifting a finger. "You are at Lady Genevieve's headquarters, the home of The Unseen. More specifically, you are in New Orleans and the year is 1967."

"New Orleans…" I said absently. "I've never been to New Orleans…or 1967."

"Well, you have now. Welcome."

"Jackson, do you know anything about what happened to Sophia?"

Jackson smiled. "You did good work with her. She's made a full recovery and is here with us as well. She isn't allowed to go home just yet. There are still some things we need to discuss, and we want to make sure she'll be safe from The Collector. And…there is something else."

"Something about Sophia? What is it?"

Jackson paused and scratched his chin. "I'll let you speak to her about that. Nothing to worry about though."

There was a quiet knock at the door and Sophia peeked

in. Her long hair seemed to enter the room before she did. "Chase? Are you awake?"

"He is," Jackson said before I could answer. "I'm sure you need some time to catch up, so I'll be on my way." He stood and turned to me before leaving. "Eat your toast," he said as he stepped out and shut the door behind him.

"Sophia, I'm so sorry about everything," I said as she sat on the bed next to me. "I never meant to get you mixed up in all of this. I had no idea this would happen — that we would end up here. I only wanted to see you one last time before the circus left town. I didn't know —"

"I know you didn't see this coming," Sophia said. She tucked her hair behind her ear. "How could you? But what I don't understand is, why me? What made The Collector think he could use me to get what he wanted from you?"

I took a sip of juice, hoping it would buy me enough time to think of an answer that wasn't entirely embarrassing. It didn't. "To tell the truth, I think The Collector thought — I mean, he believed I — I don't really know why unless — Well, he — He thought I liked you. That we were, you know, more than friends."

"Oh," Sophia said, dropping her eyes. "So he thought if he tried to hurt me that you'd protect me."

"I think so," I said. Suddenly I was aware I was in pajamas and hadn't brushed my teeth in a long time. I wasn't sure why the conversation made me so nervous, but I could feel my heart pounding and my face was red and hot.

Sophia gave a sideways glance at me. "Well, was he right? I mean, do you —"

"Chase, you're okay," Ember yelped as the door swung

open. Echo followed closely behind, practically hopping up and down from excitement. Ember brushed right past Sophia and sat on the other side of me. She grabbed me and held on like she was afraid I might disappear.

"Hi," Echo said to Sophia as he extended a hand. "I'm Echo. Nice to meet you."

"Nice to meet you too," Sophia said as she stood and returned Echo's handshake. "Hey, Chase, I'm going to go now. I'm supposed to meet with a Seer — at least I think that's the right word. Is that right? Anyway, we can talk later."

"Okay, Sophia," I said as Ember finally released her grip on me. "See you soon."

"I'm so glad you're okay," Ember said, stealing another quick hug. "Echo and I were so worried."

Echo nodded. "It's true. It's like you were in hibernation or something. Well, not really like hibernation since it was such a short period of time, relatively speaking. But it is similar since your body was attempting to regulate your temperature and slow your heart rate. Did you know woodchucks —"

"Echo," Ember interrupted. "We're all safe and together. Remember? We talked about this."

Echo put his hands up and dropped his gaze. "Got it. Safe. Together. Not the time for facts about the hibernation instincts of endothermic creatures."

"What happened to you guys?" I asked. I could feel my strength growing as each moment passed. My mind wasn't quite as foggy and my energy was returning. "Where did The Collector send you?"

"I think I was in Iceland, but I'm not sure," Ember said.

"Ironic, right? Send the fire girl to Iceland. Anyway, I wasn't there very long before Lady Genevieve showed up. I spent the night in some run-down abandoned cabin I found in the woods. Don't get me wrong, it was scary, but at least I was found quickly. Most people who end up Forsaken aren't so lucky."

"I was at a resort in the Caribbean," Echo said with a proud smile. "As soon as I realized I was on the beach, I asked a very polite man if I could use his phone. I accessed the navigation system, and poof — Bahamas, 2010. Like Ember, I wasn't there very long either." His eyes grew wide. "I saw dolphins."

Ember laughed. "Yeah, so long story short, I nearly froze to death and Echo hung out at the beach for a while."

"Did you know they found Setu?" I said. "I saw him before I healed Sophia and passed out. I'm pretty sure he helped get us away from the circus. He was able to transport us somewhere safe."

"We've been talking to Setu," Ember said. "He's been checking on you every hour or so. He's really happy to be back with people he knows."

"Do either of you know anything about Sophia?" I said. "Jackson made it seem like there's something going on with her, but he didn't give me any details."

"She was just here," Ember said, glancing toward the door. "Why didn't you ask?"

"It's no big deal. I can talk to her later."

"They think she created the storm," Ember said cutting her eyes back to me. "Apparently after Echo and I were Forsaken, there was a big storm that destroyed half the circus."

"I saw that," I said. "I was there." The memory quickly came back to me. The blood red sky. The massive streaks of lightning and the clouds that looked as if they might swallow us all. The tent ripped to shreds and the smell of smoke. "It wasn't really a storm. It looked like a storm but worse. It happened so fast, and as soon as it ended, everything went back to normal. It was like nothing had happened at all." I shook myself free of the memory. "But how is it even possible? Are you saying Sophia has an ability? That she's like us?"

Ember rolled her eyes and my guess was she didn't even realize it. "That's all we know," she said. "Maybe it wasn't her at all. Maybe it was just a weird coincidence, or someone else made it happen. They just don't know yet."

"She's meeting with the Seer now," Echo said. "It won't take long. They'll know soon if she has an ability and, if so, what it might be."

Again the door opened and our heads turned as Lady Genevieve eased into the room. "Ah, Chase, you're awake." she said. I wasn't used to someone using my full name. "It's good to see you up and about. And look, even your color is better."

"It's good to be…up," I said.

"I know you all are catching up, but I really must speak with our patient," Lady Genevieve said. "I'll make sure you have plenty of time to talk later." Ember and Echo reluctantly agreed and left the room as Echo went back to explaining woodchuck behavior to Ember.

"Lady Genevieve," I said, "before we talk I just want to say, thank you. For helping me. For rescuing Sophia. For finding Ember and Echo. And Setu. I know I can't ever repay you, but I promise I'll try."

Lady Genevieve smiled and looked at me as if she knew more about what I was thinking than I did myself. "You have been blessed with a unique gift. The simple fact that you are here and safe is repayment enough." She clapped her hands together. "Now, if you look on that table beside your bed, you'll find some clothes. Get dressed and I'll be back in a moment. I have something I want to show you."

A few minutes later I was dressed and even had time to finish my toast and juice. Lady Genevieve returned with a walking stick and a long, dark traveling cloak. The stick tapped against the wooden floor as she stepped over to me. "Chase, I want to take you somewhere. It's a special place to me. Somewhere quiet where we can talk and not have to worry about interruptions or prying ears. Would you accompany me?" I nodded and Lady Genevieve reached out to me. As soon as I touched her warm, weathered hand, the world went dark. When I opened my eyes, we were standing in the middle of a cool desert just as the sun was beginning to set over the dunes. The sky was filled with large puffs of clouds that reflected deep shades of red and purple, turning to a brilliant golden glow just at the point where sky met desert. It was peaceful. Beautiful. In the still silence of that moment, Lady Genevieve stood facing the sun, its golden rays bathing her face in a solemn glow. Her eyes were closed, and she was lost in her own serene thoughts.

"What do you think?" she asked as her eyes cracked open.

"It's amazing. Where are we?"

Lady Genevieve pointed over her shoulder, and I turned

to behold a sight that would be etched into my memories for the rest of my life. Three large pyramids and a sphinx, sitting like kings of stone on the sandy earth. The Pyramids of Giza and the Great Sphinx. It was them and us. No one else was around. There were no tourists or archaeologists. No travelers or even locals. There was only Lady Genevieve, me, and the ancient tombs that rose from the desert sands.

"No matter how many times I see this, it never fails to impress." Lady Genevieve said. "This is a special place to me. I find it helps keeps me centered. It reminds me of my limitations and my human fragility."

"Are we in the present?" I asked.

"Goodness, no," Lady Genevieve answered. "The year is 1763, long before patrols, tourists, and photographers were trudging around the site." She jabbed her walking stick into the sand and leaned against it. "You know what I appreciate most about them?" she said, motioning to the pyramids. "It's the fact that they are beyond my reach."

"What do you mean? I didn't think anything was out of your reach — or The Collector's either."

"Our abilities are like muscles. The more we exercise them, the stronger they become. I've been traveling through space and times for decades now — far longer than The Collector even. It has become second nature to me. I do it with little thought or effort. But I do have my limits. We all do."

"Limits? You mean, you can't go to any time or place you want?"

Lady Genevieve nodded. "That's right. The further I travel, or the longer I stay, the more energy it uses. My farthest trip was to the Roman province of Thracia in AD 378.

I witnessed the Battle of Adrianople. It was both fascinating and brutal. A sight to behold. Unfortunately, the journey nearly killed me. I managed to make it home, but I lay in a coma for nearly a week. I haven't attempted a trip of that distance since."

"So, The Collector, he has limits too?"

"He does, and that is exactly what is driving him mad." Lady Genevieve paused and pursed her lips as if she was trying to figure out how to make sense of it for me. "Imagine if your friends went on a trip, but you weren't able to go. And, upon their return, they talked about how much fun they had and how they wished you could have been with them." I nodded, listening intently and doing my best to pay attention. To understand. "And, because you felt left out, you came to me and asked if I'd send you back in time so you could experience the trip with your friends."

"I never thought of that. That would be great."

"How many times would you be able to relive that experience?"

For some reason, I wanted Lady Genevieve to think I was smart, so I thought carefully before answering. "I guess… just the once? Every day for the week, right?"

"How did you come to that conclusion?"

It wasn't clear if she was impressed or not. "Well, if I joined them every day, then I was already *there*. I did everything there was to do. If I went back and tried to do it again later, there would be two of me there. That would just be weird, and I'm not even sure if it's possible. But it seems like I'd only get the one chance."

Lady Genevieve dropped her eyes and smiled. It was a

weary smile. One that seemed full of pain or perhaps regret. "Very good, Chase. Now imagine if that trip was the last opportunity you'd ever have to see your friends."

"That would be terrible. I'd want to travel back and see them as much as I could."

"And now you know how The Collector feels." Lady Genevieve took a settling breath and adjusted her weight on the walking stick. "The Collector, or James, is running out of time. More accurately, he's running out of days. Lynette, the woman you saw from the memory stone, passed away from what they referred to as consumption. She died in 1808. James met the young woman in 1801 while on an errand for the council. It wasn't until near the end of her life that they became romantically involved although The Council warned him against such a relationship. Not only are Time Travelers prohibited from becoming romantically involved with anyone from the past, they are also forbidden from bringing anyone from the past to the present for purely personal gain. While we weren't able to stop him from becoming involved with Lynette, the council asked me to use my abilities to keep her tethered to her own time."

"And since The Collector can't bring her to the present, he isn't able to save her," I said quietly as Lady Genevieve agreed. "And if he can't save her while she's there, and he can't bring her to the present, he only has so many days to spend with her. She'd be too young if he visited too early and he can't overlap his visits. Just like we talked about with my friends and the trip."

"The Collector is angry and hurt," she said. "James isn't a bad person. He isn't evil. He is simply grieving the loss of someone he believes he has the ability to save, were it allowed. It's a terrible hurt to endure. As a Traveler, I know very well the pain he lives with. On top of that, James is getting older and his days of being with Lynette are numbered. He's desperate."

"Which is why he needs me."

"Exactly. If he is unable to bring Lynette into the present to be treated, he needs a Healer to go back with him and remove the illness from her. Healers are few and far between. Very few have ever existed as far as we know. The odds were against him, but he found you, and he needs you."

"Couldn't he just take a doctor back with him? Why does it have to be me?"

"He has attempted to find physicians to support him. However, without modern equipment or medicine, the doctors didn't do him much good. Even when he was able to explain himself — to help those men and women understand his ability and situation, most of them refused to help. Sadly, some of them ended up Forsaken as a result. Even those who tried to help told him Lynette would need to be in a modern facility if she even had a hope of recovery. Several attempts have been made. All have failed. James needs more than a doctor. He needs a Healer."

As angry as I was, a large part of me felt sorry for The Collector. He brought me into his family. Whether or not it was for selfish purposes, didn't change the fact that my friends were in my life because of him. The pain of wanting what you can't have is one I understood. "This whole thing… it isn't over, is it?"

"I'm afraid not, Chase."

"What do we do now?"

"For now, we wait. I'll report back to the council and we'll devise a plan of action." Lady Genevieve reached into her pocket and pulled out a sandy, red stone. "This is for you," she said as she passed it to me.

"Is this a memory stone?" I asked.

"It is. Whenever you find the need to settle your mind, simply use the stone and it will bring you back here. Everyone needs a refuge."

"Thank you," I said as I slipped the stone into my pocket. "Lady Genevieve? I heard that Sophia may have caused the storm back at the circus. Ember said you think she may have abilities. Is that true?"

"We aren't sure yet," Lady Genevieve said as she shifted her weight on the walking stick. "Something unusual happened for sure. And we know it wasn't any of our people. But don't worry. We'll know soon."

"If she does have an ability, will she have to stay here with —"

"We will know soon," Lady Genevieve cut in. "And we will make sure all of you are safe."

Lady Genevieve and I stood there side by side staring at the pyramids for a while. Those endless sands stretched on as far as I could see, and the great stone structures were turning purple against the horizon. As the sun dipped beneath the sand I couldn't help but think about all that had happened. All that had changed. I thought about how fragile and small our lives are and how easily we could be here one moment and gone the next. Forgotten. I was as unsure about the future as I had ever been, but I knew I had a gift, I knew who my friends were, and I knew that difficult times were ahead no matter how hard I tried to avoid them. It had been nearly two years since I'd become one of The Lost. But that time and that life had become my past.

ABOUT THE AUTHOR

Ken Nobles has a Bachelor of Arts in Biblical Studies and English from William Carey University and a Masters in Christian Education from Southwestern Baptist Theological Seminary. He has taught Bible, English, and creative writing to high school students for nearly twenty years. Ken currently lives in Hudson Oaks, Texas with his wife, Gretchen and serves as the Secondary Principal at Trinity Christian Academy.

www.ingramcontent.com/pod-product-compliance
Lightning Source LLC
Chambersburg PA
CBHW020612180626
46810CB00007B/2746